ALSO BY JASON REYNOLDS

Ain't Burned All the Bright

All American Boys (cowritten with Brendan Kiely)

As Brave As You

The Boy in the Black Suit

For Every One

Long Way Down

Look Both Ways

Miles Morales: Spider-Man

My Name is Jason. Mine Too.

Stamped: Racism, Antiracism, and You (cowritten with Ibram X. Kendi)

Stuntboy, in the Meantime

When I Was the Greatest

The Track Series:

Ghost

Patina

Sunny

Lu

MARVEL

MILES MORALES

A SPIDER-MAN NOVEL

JASON REYNOLDS
ILLUSTRATIONS BY ZEKE PEÑA

A A CAITLYN DLOUHY BOOK
atheneum   NEW YORK LONDON TORONTO SYDNEY NEW DELHI

An imprint of Simon & Schuster Children's Publishing Division
1230 Avenue of the Americas, New York, New York 10020

Text by Jason Reynolds
Illustration by Zeke Peña
Jacket design by Simon & Schuster, Inc.
Quotation on page 50 is from Laurie Halse Anderson's discussion of censorship at the American Booksellers Foundation for Free Expression seminar, Feb 2013.

For information about special discounts for bulk purchases, please contact Simon & Schuster Special Sales at 1-866-506-1949 or business@simonandschuster.com.
The Simon & Schuster Speakers Bureau can bring authors to your live event. For more information or to book an event, contact the Simon & Schuster Speakers Bureau at 1-866-248-3049 or visit our website at www.simonspeakers.com.
The text for this book was set in Cronos Pro and ITC New Baskerville Std.
The illustrations for this book were rendered digitally.
Manufactured in the United States of America
First Edition
2 4 6 8 10 9 7 5 3 1
CIP data for this book is available from the Library of Congress.
ISBN 9781665918466
ISBN 9781665918480 (ebook)

For Adrian
—J. R.

For Diego
—Z. P.

MILES MORALES

SUSPENDED

A SPIDER-MAN NOVEL

Perhaps I stand on the brink of a great discovery, and perhaps after I have made my great discovery I will be sent home in chains.

—**Jamaica Kincaid,** from "Wingless"

SPIDER FACT

It's said
that nobody
is ever more
than ten feet
from a spider.

They be everywhere
you and me are.

And even though
we see them only
when they
big enough
to see, or when
they move,
like a cursor
across the blank white
page of a wall,

or when we trip
the web-like wire
of a booby trap,

or when they
fang our flesh,

we should probably
assume most

just be right there,
right here,
looking at us,
looking over them.

———————————

Miles Morales has had quite a week.

(QUITE A) WEEK IN REVIEW (SORT OF):

Last MONDAY, Miles received a letter from his cousin, Austin. From jail. Miles never even knew Austin existed. (More on this later.)

TUESDAY, Miles was accused of stealing sausages from his campus job. Yes . . . sausages. He was in the dean's office with his parents, on the brink of expulsion. Fortunately, that didn't happen. *Phew.* An extra life. (More on this later.)

Later that day, still angry about the accusation and disgusted by his racist history teacher, Mr. Chamberlain, Miles, unaware of his own strength, accidentally broke his desk in history class. But that's as far as he went.

The next day, WEDNESDAY, Miles's crush, Alicia Carson, also Black, also in Chamberlain's class, also upset about the teacher's racist rants, staged a protest in the middle of the "history lesson" and was suspended. (More on this later.)

SATURDAY, Miles's father took him to a correctional facility to see Austin. (More on this later.)

That night, the school threw a Halloween party. Two things happened: (1) Miles made his move and gave Alicia a poem he'd written for her. And (2) Miles, full of suspicion—his Spidey Sense had been wonky all week—snuck away and discovered the villain of all villains, the Warden, who also happened to be connected to Miles's history teacher. The racist one. (More on this later.)

SUNDAY, he defeated the Warden. (More on this later.)

When Miles got back to his dorm, his best friend and roommate, Ganke, gave him a poem left for him by Alicia. Yes, *that* Alicia. It was in response to the poem Miles had written her. (More on this later.)

MONDAY in history class, Mr. Chamberlain told Miles he had to sit on the floor—*the floor!*—the duration of the class since Miles had broken his desk a few days before. (More on this later.)

Miles refuses.   (More on this now.)

ON DAYS LIKE TODAY (TUESDAY)

I wish I was:

>   looked over,
>   looked at,
>   looked in,
>   looked like.

Anything
other than

>   locked up.

_____

Okay, not exactly "locked up," but definitely locked *in*.

IN-SCHOOL SUSPENSION

I'm only here
for telling the truth.

I'm only here
because when you

upset or upstage or
upside-down

any authority figures,
like teachers who

can't figure out who
you are but think

they know who you are,
and don't know you

know who you are,
they name you a

bigmouth boy,
a trouble, a lie.

It could be said, depending on who you ask, that Miles is the bearer of good conscience. It could also be said that he's a magnet for bad luck. What else would be the reason he landed himself in In-School Suspension after telling Mr. Chamberlain he was not going to put up with his crap anymore, besides telling Mr. Chamberlain he was not going to put up with his crap anymore? Well, that's not exactly how Miles worded it, but it was definitely the gist of what he'd shouted. While sitting at the *teacher's* desk. In the middle of class.

But who could blame the kid? Mr. Chamberlain had been disrespecting Miles all quarter and finally pushed him too far: tried to make him small by ordering him to sit on the floor—again . . . the *floor!*—to do his classwork. And Miles, drowning in embarrassment and fuming with anger, went off. Told Mr. Chamberlain he was not (1) a pincushion, or (2) a punching bag, or (3) a puppet, or (4) a pet, or (5) a pawn. None of those things.

But the truth about Brooklyn Visions Academy is that, here, sometimes Miles felt like *all* those things.

MY BROOKLYN

And even though
I *am* a bigmouth boy
and *can* be trouble,
I ain't no troublemaker
and I ain't no lie.

And just because I'm
at this fancy school,
Brooklyn Visions Academy,
don't mean I ain't the
vision of a different Brooklyn

where we talk loud enough
to be heard over car horns
on Fulton Street, or the grind
of the A train against the rails,
or the sirens, red, white, and blue

lights flashing in our eyes.
Little girls flash smiles at
their flashy older sisters,
doobie-wrapped and
trash-talking geniuses in

tights and sneaks. Little boys
flash middle fingers because
it's funny, and their older
brothers' lives flash before
their eyes before their time.

And the sidewalk's like a runway
for whatever's fly at the moment,
and also the possibility
we just might lift off and
take flight at any time.

There was a stark difference between Miles's school and his block. Brooklyn Visions Academy was a boarding school or, as Miles called it, a "bored-ing" school, which meant the students actually stayed on campus. Ate there. Slept there. Which meant they lived at school, a concept only a lunatic could've come up with. Of course, this was also the basic premise of college, which technically was what this school was supposed to be preparing its students for. A pipeline. But Miles was sixteen, and at sixteen, *nothing* sounds worse than living at school. Especially when you're from where Miles is from.

MY BLOCK

Morning is for the birds.
And the buses.
And the occasional
chunky heel clacking
toward the workday.
And the call to prayer.
And the raucous rattle
of security gates lifting.
And eyelids lifting to meet
a sun that barely breaks
the brownstone roofline.
Everything orange.

Afternoon is for the birds.
The pigeons picking at
pizza and leftover heroes.
Crosswalks like drawbridges
for the fresh-outta-school
and the old ladies coming
from rubbing pennies
against scratch-offs before
the kids rule the bodega,
buggin' out, talking tough
like smiles are a dead giveaway,
but not juice stains or barrettes.

Night. Is for the birds.

On Miles's block there was Ms. Shine, a woman who faithfully got up every day to water the flowers she'd carefully planted in beds in front of her house. Everyone knew she was waiting for her son, Cyrus, to return home, though no one knew where he'd gone. Somewhere high, somewhere low. And Mr. Frankie, the block's handyman, always covered in dust or paint. A walking abstract art piece. And Fat Tony, who sat on his stoop all day bumming cigarettes and stealing lighters. Only dude in the neighborhood with a basset hound. And a young woman named Frenchie who managed the dollar store like it was a million-dollar store. Or her son, Martell, who was probably one of the best ball players in Brooklyn. At least that's what Frenchie hoped. Or Neek, who had seen more than anyone would ever know—war, *real* war—and peeked at the block through the blinds of his apartment as if waiting for a tank to roll by.

And, of course, Rio and Jeff, Miles's mom and dad.

HOME

My mother
keep a bodega
hanging off her shoulder.
And I swear my pop's
the chin-up champ.

I'm from them.
I'm from there.
That's my Brooklyn,
and I'm Miles
away from home.

———————

Miles was the perfect combination of them both. His mother's ability to make much out of the minuscule, his father's ability to keep his head up regardless of the weight he kept tucked under his Yankee fitted.

Boricua and Black and Brooklyn as hell.

HERE

Ain't no uniforms here, but this school
still feels buttoned-up button-up. Still
feels like a button-down collar, a blazer too tight
in the shoulders, all structure, no place
for movement. No wiggle room or flare or flavor.

This school feels like loafers in lockstep,
even though I'm more sneakers, loose laced,
tongue out, scholarship-bopping like
one foot on the sidewalk, and one in the street.

Most days I just wear a T-shirt and hoodie,
and it still feels like a tie around my neck,
with the Windsor knot my father taught me
to tie for church. But his way always
leaves space to undo the top button
and breathe some. But not here. Not at

this school. Here, the knot, though invisible,
is tight tight and pressed right up
against my voice box so I can barely
speak. And if I do say something, every
word gotta fight its way outta me,
outta my oil slick of a neck, because they be
sweating and sweating me like I ain't cool.

Yes, Boricua and Black and Brooklyn as hell, but that didn't necessarily mean Miles was oozing with what some of the men in his neighborhood had. What his dad and his uncle Aaron had. Guys like them seemed to have subway tracks running down their forearms. Cab smoke in their lungs. The types of fellas who styled and smiled like they were addicted to floss, whose hands curved just the right way for dap to feel and look and sound like an extension of their natural *hi*.

That wasn't Miles. He had something, for sure. But not that.

AND FORREAL, I AIN'T COOL

But I am me.
　　Before here.

Before the hallways
　　and the bunkbeds.

Before the millions of
　　million-pound textbooks.

Before the delicious food (pizza)
　　and the disgusting food (pizza with pineapple).

Before the passionate teachers
　　and the paychecked terrors,

and even the spider bite,
　　and the itchy scar it left behind.

I been me.
　　Been.

However, Miles did have *something* "cool" about him. He might not have called it that, but Ganke definitely would've. And the evidence of it was an irritated hand. A dime-size scar, slightly raised.

You probably already know the story, but in case you don't, Miles was hanging out with his uncle Aaron some years back—his favorite uncle—when he was bitten by a radioactive spider. Yes, yes, like another not-so-cool kid. And from there, like that other kid, Miles . . . changed.

He could climb walls. (Sticky fingers.)
He could leap strangely high. (With chicken legs.)
He had superhuman strength. (And noodle arms.)
He could camouflage himself. (As in, disappear.)
He could send electric current through his fingers. (Vibes.)
He could shoot web. (He . . . had web-shooters.)

And still looked just like regular ol' not-so-cool Miles.

So, yeah . . . cool. In a different way.

TO REITERATE

And that's why I ain't got
a whole lot of time for

no authority figures,
like teachers who

can't figure out who
I am but think

they know who I am,
and don't know I

know who I am,
so they name me

an ungrateful mess,
a snowflake, a brat.

Miles also wasn't the toughest kid. Not the type to throw himself in front of the drama train or run toward the controversy storm. If anything, he always tried his best to stay away from it all. To lie low. To just get his work done as best he could and make it to the weekend so he could cut loose from what was blocking him and get back to his block. And breathe.

SNOWFLAKES

But the thing about
snowflakes

is that they're distinct, like
fingerprints.

Sure, they're collectively
beautiful

but individually special, like
cobwebs.

But despite Miles's preference to lie low, his mother and father raised him to stand up for himself.

Brooklyn—*his* Brooklyn—taught him to do the same.

HISTORY CLASS

You ever had
a teacher

who taught you
like they

were teaching
you a lesson?

This is how it all started. Everything was fine—or at least as fine as things could be for Miles at Brooklyn Visions Academy—until he started taking Mr. Chamberlain's class. Fourth period. To say Mr. Chamberlain taught history would be giving him too much credit. Mr. Chamberlain *was* history. A piece of parched parchment. He was a teacher stuck in the 1700s, teaching American history as if it were a story of only triumph and honor. As if the American flag hadn't been used for tug-o'-war. As if slavery wasn't . . .

slavery.

Miles thought, either Mr. Chamberlain had reached that age where his mind had started to spoil, or . . . Mr. Chamberlain's mind was being controlled by a man—an *idea?* a *monster?*—who was hundreds of years old. His name: the Warden.

(Yes, I know this is hard to believe, but haven't we all bought into more unbelievable things?)

See, a few days ago—Saturday—Miles found an underground tunnel stretching from Brooklyn Visions Academy to the King's County Department of Corrections. And just beyond the jail was a big house, complete with pillars and porch, massive windows, and wood that had been burrowed through by termites. Hollow but still standing. In that big house lived the Warden, who attacked Miles (after Miles showed up on his doorstep clearly not looking for a cup of sugar) and even ordered *all* his minions—the Chamberlains, zombies in the shapes of teachers who were ushering Black and Brown kids from schools to jails through unfair disciplinary measures—to ambush Miles. To shut him up. To shut him down.

To destroy him.

But Miles . . . *ahem* . . . Spider-Man prevailed. Not the easiest victory, but a victory nonetheless. And afterward, Miles figured that since he'd taken out the Warden, he'd also freed Mr. Chamberlain, *all* the Chamberlains, of the Warden's bigoted mind control. Because you know what they say about chopping off the head of the snake . . . No? . . . You don't? Well, it doesn't matter anyway, because

turned out Mr. Chamberlain was just an asshole.

THE WARDEN: A DESCRIPTION

All I know is, for some reason,
this four-hundred-year-old
wanted to flush me down,
flush me through a pristine
pipeline. Ain't no rust
or crust on it or nothing
despite it being older than
old. It shines like it's new.
It works like it is, too.
And this four-hundred-year-old
monster who wanted me to go
from pupil to prisoner,
from student to statistic, used
it as a damn drinking straw.

The Warden had not only controlled the minds of thousands of teachers over the course of decades—even Miles's father and all his friends had dealt with different Chamberlains when they were young, teachers who unfairly punished them until they were forced out of school and into a life of crime—but he also got into Miles's head, too. Gave him nightmares. Hauntings of his dead uncle, Aaron.

In the nightmares, Miles's uncle would taunt him, telling Miles he was just like him. A future criminal. That his destiny was a dirty one. But this was all the Warden's doing. Miles knew his uncle was much more than felonies and jail bids. Their relationship was pizza in the projects. Laughter and bad advice about how to get girls. Never about crime.

Also, never about Uncle Aaron's son, Austin.

AUSTIN DAVIS (LONG-LOST COUSIN): A DESCRIPTION

Skin the color of grease in the Bustelo can my mother keeps on the stove.
A little bit more hair than a little bit. Probably brushes for waves.
He talks like his tongue is a dull razor blade. But still Brooklyn-sharp.
And aside from his khaki shirt and khaki pants—his ugly uniform—

he's pretty.
Much.

Like me.

———————

Except for the fact that Austin was incarcerated. So . . . not exactly
like Miles, though, again, Miles often thought of his school like jail.
But it wasn't.

Miles received a letter from Austin last Monday. Austin had tracked Miles's address down through his grandmother and just wanted to connect and also clear the air about his father, Miles's uncle, Aaron, who Miles's father resented for not leaving their lives as crooks behind them.

The day before fighting the Warden, Miles and his father went to the detention center to meet Austin. This was also the day Miles had given Alicia the poem he'd written for her, just three lines about how she smelled like sandalwood, which was true but . . . a little creepy. Had he known Austin better and had Austin not been locked up, Miles could've probably asked him for advice about it all. Like he used to do Uncle Aaron. Maybe Austin could've given Miles a way to flirt without admitting he'd been obsessing about her for weeks. But the truth was, Miles's visit to the jail had been wrapped up in too many other questions. Too many other things he'd been sniffing out.

Why have we never met?
Why did our fathers not get along?
Why did my father make it out of the street and yours didn't?
When do you get out?
Will you send me another letter?
What do you do for fun in here?
What books do y'all have in here?
What books do you want in here?
Will they let me bring books in here?
Why are we having the same nightmares?
How did you end up here?
Why does the guard keep yelling at us?
And why does that guard have the same name as my . . . history teacher?

MR. CHAMBERLAIN: A DESCRIPTION

A statue pretending to be a statue
of a severely unhappy person,
face whittled from rotten wood, carved
with a sledgehammer and classroom key
as if someone or something had decided
ugly and unkind should be on display,
unfinished and unpolished, but labeled
a masterpiece.

And Mr. Chamberlain had the nerve to say in class that during American chattel slavery, the relationship between enslaver and the enslaved person was actually a healthy, oftentimes happy one. He said it was no different than owner and dog, that dogs didn't mind leashes, or cages, or even scraps to eat, and that despite those things, they always wagged their tails, happy to see the people who owned them.

See? Asshole.

HISTORY CLASS

You ever had
a teacher

who taught you
like *student*

was a synonym
for *stupid*?

_____

AIN'T GONNA
HAPPEN . . .

The answer, for Miles, was yes. He absolutely knew what that was like.

So much so that last TUESDAY he broke his own desk. There's only so much a kid (with superpowers) can take.

WEDNESDAY, he had sat at that broken desk, wobbly legs and everything. Did the best he could.

THURSDAY and FRIDAY, the wobbly legs had been removed, and the desktop sat on the floor.

"We just don't damage things and act like we didn't. We have to live with that. *You* have to live with that," Mr. Chamberlain had said yesterday, MONDAY, now ordering Miles to sit on the linoleum by the legless desk.

But to Mr. Chamberlain's surprise, only the desk was broken. *Miles's* legs weren't wobbly. At all.

WHAT LANDED ME HERE

I told him:

We are not pincushions.
We are not punching bags.
We are not puppets.
We are not pets.
We are not pawns.

We are people.
We are people.
We are people.

We told him.

In a school like Brooklyn Visions Academy, desks are easily replaceable. Dignity is not.

So instead of Miles allowing himself to be treated like an animal, he began spouting a manifesto Alicia had taught him. One she and the whole class joined in chanting.

We are not pincushions. We are not punching bags. We are not puppets. . . .

IN TROUBLE

He told us
to stand down,
to stand up.

That we
were trouble
and in trouble.

That we'd
gone too far.
To get out.

———————

So they got out. Marched out.

Kicked out.

INEVITABLE

The campus police met us in the hallway.
I knew they'd come for us. I knew I'd
said what needed to be said, did what
needed to be done, and now I would pay.

They did not touch me. Just walked alongside
me to the dean's office, where my conscience
would be questioned in a way I knew
my consequence would never be.

Though the path to the dean's office was lined with the most beautiful oak trees and azalea bushes and other kinds of plants only the science teachers and landscapers could name, it was rarely a pleasant journey.

Miles had just taken it six days before. He knew there was never enough trees to distract from the trouble.

SIX DAYS BEFORE or CAMPUS (IN)CONVENIENCE or SAUSAGE IN A CAN

I still can't believe
the last time I took this walk
to Kushner's office,

it was because I was accused
of stealing a whole bunch
of cans of sausage.

There's a stupid joke in there
somewhere, but there was
nothing funny

about my mother's face
as she held her breath
and waited for the dean

to dish out my verdict.
Can you imagine sausage
being the sucker punch

that knocks the wind out
your chances? Cheap cans of can't,
spoiling your appetite?

CAMPUS CONVENIENCE:
Notebooks, pencils, pens, hole punchers, staplers, paper clips, noodles, stale snack cakes, and sausage in a can. So, nothing any teenager would want (except maybe the noodles).

So why would Miles pinch a bunch of cans of sausage? He wouldn't. He didn't. Not to mention he needed his job as a cashier in the store—work study—because without it, his parents would be on the hook for room and board, and they didn't have that kind of money. As a matter of fact, Miles didn't even know he'd been accused until he made it to the dean's office. He found out later that Mr. Chamberlain had stolen them to set him up. Weird, but true.

Fortunately for Miles, there was no proof that he'd done anything wrong. No surveillance footage of any infraction. So . . . no evidence, no expulsion.

SPIDER FACT

Did you know
American tarantulas

use their hair as weaponry?

Tiny needles turned knives.
Follicles that be fierce and feared.

This time, in the waiting area outside the dean's office, Miles knew exactly what he was there for. He brushed his hair with the palm of his hand, tried to lay it down like his mother did when he was a little boy or whenever he'd gone too long without a cut. She called it "cleaning himself up." His father called it "freshening." But Miles never felt dirty or spoiled. Scared? Maybe. But never dirty, and never spoiled.

Through the dean's door, Miles could hear the murmurs of a heated conversation.

"I'm trying to understand why my child, Reggie, who is a senior here, can't seem to find the necessary information in your library to write their senior research paper. Do you know how much money it costs to go here?"

"Yes ma'am, I do. And I assure you—"

"Then why can't they find any work on Harvey Milk? Why can't they find any work on Stonewall? On Marsha P. Johnson?"

"There's been some issues, but we're trying to rectify them now, but—"

"There will always be issues, Dean Kushner. But surely you'd agree we're supposed to be providing them information to help them grow into much better people than we are, no?"

WAITING

I stare at the floor, the
shiny planks of red

wood, the lacquer dulled
from being all-day-long

walked on, the knots
like curious eyes staring up at me,

recognizing something familiar.
Something else splintered.

Miles walked his eyes along the molding, an extra piece of wood that looked like a railing too small to hold, that cut the wall in half, gave it some dimension. All the old brownstones in Brooklyn had different kinds of molding, including Miles's house. In this moment, Miles imagined himself miniature, running along it. Imagined himself on a ledge.

Where the molding met the corner, Miles noticed a tiny pile of what seemed to be dirt. Maybe sawdust. Something like that. Curious, he leaned over to dab it away with his finger as if his mother was right there in the seat next to him telling him to take pride in his work whenever he was dusting the house. As if she was reminding him that a mess ain't nothing but a message. Usually, when she said this, she meant the message was for him to not wait for her to clean. To take it upon himself to tidy his environment.

But before he could swipe it away—because boredom and anxiety will make you do such things—before he could add it to the rest of the dust in the air, the dean's door opened.

"I just want them to be better than us." A woman dressed in a suit came storming out. Miles could tell by the look on her face that she was furious. "They deserve it!"

DEAN KUSHNER'S OFFICE

I'm sitting here surrounded by all this leather,
all this wood, the ornate edges of history,
the shaky shelves jammed with dusty
books, tissue-paper pages like the family
Bible where Abuela keeps all the Morales
secrets. Again. I stare at the one bright spot
on the dean's bald head, the perfect landing
pad for a spider. But they are all busy in the
corners, weaving something magnificent,
something delicate and tough, something
complicated. Somewhere hidden, spinning
poems from their abdomens, survival kits.
Whole worlds happening in the dark spots,
in the crevices of all this smart talk about
how much of an opportunity this is for
me to be here and how I shouldn't throw
it all away just because I want to prove a
point and how will my parents afford this
if I lose my scholarship? And how will they
ever forgive me? And how will I ever forgive
myself? And how will I ever make it in the
world if I don't learn to keep quiet and
kiss the hand that sometimes slaps me down?

Miles looked around Dean Kushner's office as the dean punched numbers on the phone. And as he called Miles's parents, Miles glanced at the leather-bound copies of Shakespeare and Hemingway and Faulkner and Chaucer, none of which he was familiar with besides Shakespeare. Miles had read *Macbeth* and loved it because he felt like he could relate. He hadn't received a premonition from three witches who told him he'd be king of Scotland—Miles knew nothing of Scotland—but he had been bitten by a spider that made him feel like he could be king of Brooklyn. Sort of. Maybe more like knight of Brooklyn. There were also old books on wars and war heroes. The point is, leather makes everything seem more serious. Miles even thought about possibly adding a leather jacket to his wardrobe, a style recommendation from Ganke. But all that was interrupted by Miles landing on a beautiful book positioned face-out on the shelf. It was about Samuel Morse and the invention of the telegraph. Miles wished he could send a telegraph to his parents about this so he wouldn't have to hear their voices, but then *that* thought was interrupted, too, once he heard static in the tone of his father's voice on the other end of the phone.

"Good afternoon, sir," the dean said. "This is Dean Kushner from Brooklyn Visions Academy." Dean Kushner put the phone on speaker.

"O . . . kay." Miles's father's voice plunked into a sea of concern. "What's going on?"

"I hate to call you with such inconvenient news, especially since we just rectified the, uh, sausage situation a few days ago. But I assure you we have it all under control. I just wanted to inform you that Miles will be in In-School Suspension tomorrow."

VERSIONS

That afternoon Ganke comes busting into the room
all huffy because he's heard about what happened
and can't wait to hear it from me. But not before
he tells me all the different versions of the story.
Because school is all about versions of a story.

"Yo, I heard you told him you wasn't a pincushion and then you picked up the desk and cracked it over his old-ass head!" Ganke howled.

"Then I heard you broke out in a rap about equal rights, which didn't really sound like something you'd do, but you've been wildin' lately, so maybe you got bars and I didn't know, even though I would know because I've been your best friend for five hundred years and I freestyle all the time and you never join in. But whatever," Ganke added.

"Also, I heard when you were telling him all the things you weren't—that you even told him you wasn't a Pepsi that he could just guzzle and belch up—you were crying a little bit, and you raised your fist slowly like you were in a movie," Ganke went on, playing out the scene.

"Oh, and my favorite was that you slapped Mr. Chamberlain in the face, and his nose came off. And then you picked it up off the floor and used it as chalk and started writing your speech on the board with it. *I am not a pineapple. I am not a persimmon. I am not a pomegranate*," Ganke finished.

"And what's a pincushion?" Ganke asked.

Miles didn't answer, though he was sort of amused Ganke knew what a persimmon was but not a pincushion.

"Your parents know all this happened?" Ganke squinted, almost bracing himself.

"Yeah." Finally, a word.

"What they say?" Ganke took a seat on his bed. He'd been so riled up that he hadn't even taken his backpack off.

Miles didn't respond. Just lay back and pulled his pillow over his head.

WHAT MY PARENTS SAID:

Listen,

(*sigh sigh sigh*)

son,

(*sigh sigh sigh*)

just

(*sigh sigh sigh*)

keep

(*sigh sigh sigh*)

trying.

———————

They told Miles they weren't upset.
They told Miles they believed him.
They told Miles they would've done the same thing.
They told Miles they were proud.

And then:

They told Miles to just   keep   trying.
And it sounded like,   *Do*   *your*   *time.*

SPIDER FACT

Spiders have so many eyes.
  Some eight,
others as many as twelve.

But not a single eyelid.

So spiders don't never close
  their eyes,
awake even while asleep.

———————

Miles got this book, an old flimsy paperback called *Arachnophilia: The Strange and Unbelievable World of Spiders*, from the school library last week. He'd ventured in there, embarrassed and frustrated, after his parents had left the conference with the dean. Again . . . over stolen sausages. He'd been in the library before, but on this day, it had felt different. The library at Brooklyn Visions Academy was big and warm and had the leather and wood, copper grommets and rivets, and all the sophisticated craftsmanship of an old building. As if the woodworkers were trying to make a monument out of cursive writing. The banisters all curled. Pillars like t's crossed with intricately decorated beams. It was like every library should be, a place of wonder. A respite for the restless mind. Perfect for Miles.

Because Mrs. Tripley, the librarian, had been on a ladder when Miles had arrived, she and Miles had quickly gotten caught up in small talk about superstition, sparking Miles to ask if she knew of any superstitions about spiders.

"It used to be said that spiders could connect the past with the future," Mrs. Tripley had said. And when Miles came back to the library, frazzled after breaking his desk in Mr. Chamberlain's class, Tripley led him through the stacks. She stopped at a particular shelf, reached into the row, and snatched a book from its place so confidently that it was impossible for Miles to not wonder if she knew where every book in the library was.

She handed Miles the book. He hadn't requested it, but that's how librarians are, doling out books like church candy. Which is probably how she got kids like Tobin Rogers to work for her.

Tobin was an awkward, big-headed kid with too many teeth, who worked as a library assistant. A birthmark all across his face like a spill. Glasses thick as Plexi backboard. Lips over-licked, leaving a burn around his mouth. He was only a few paces from Miles, crawling around a mess of books, putting some back on the bottom shelf.

"Don't dog-ear the pages, please," he said softly to Miles who had only been holding the spider book for, maybe, five seconds. Definitely not long enough to do any damage.

Mrs. Tripley looked at Miles, shrugged. "Another superstition.

Tobin loves books so much, he gets upset when you bend the corners. He's a bit of a purist, which kinda makes him the best library assistant ever." Miles knew Tobin. Knew him to be, sort of, an everything-nerd. Mathlete. Chess team. And was even captain of the history club. Miles knew all this because he had been recruited for all these clubs even though Miles didn't love math, was decent at chess (thanks to the barbershop), and hated history, or at least history *class* thanks to Mr. Chamberlain, who happened to be the advisor for the history club. But . . . diversity, diversity, diversity.

"What happens if I do?" Miles asked, expecting Tobin to give him some type of scientific answer.

"Don't," Tobin said, sliding a book between two others in the stack.

"But . . . how will I keep my place?" Miles asked. But to that, Tobin didn't respond.

Now, had there been a spider club, Miles might've been game. Especially since he was all in this new book and learning all these new facts. He'd had his nose buried in it every night before bed, and kept it stuffed down in his back pocket just in case he could carve out a moment to peek at a new tidbit, hoping it would illuminate something he hadn't quite learned about himself. His *new* self.

Ganke, on the other hand, didn't understand why Miles's new self didn't want to play video games or gossip about how it was almost a guarantee that Winston Faulk was going to punch Brock Hanky in the face over a bad joke at the Halloween party, and why he was reading a book as nightmarish as one about spiders. Before bed. The last thing Ganke wanted was to dream about eight-legged critters. He also didn't want that for Miles because he dreaded waking up and finding his best friend stuck to the ceiling after a night of sleep-crawling. It had happened before, and it wasn't okay.

RESTLESS

When I can't sleep,
I chase my nightmares

out my head.
Out my bed

into the night, where
they live wild and free.

Until they meet me.

———————

Ganke fell asleep with his blanket completely over his head, but
Miles couldn't seem to get himself to settle down. Couldn't get his

brain to take a break. He was thinking about everything that had happened in class, but also about what his father was *really* thinking after the call from Dean Kushner. Though he'd said he was proud of Miles for standing up for what was right, Miles couldn't help but think about the way his father had completely disconnected from his own brother, Uncle Aaron. How he'd judged Aaron for his life in crime without ever considering that maybe, just maybe, Aaron was doing what was necessary to take care of his family.

Miles was also doing the best he could, not necessarily to take care of his family, but definitely to make them proud. But if it didn't look the way Miles's father wanted it to look, would he disown Miles, too? Miles didn't think so, but still . . . the thought of it kept him up.

So, Miles suited up. Pulled the uniform on, rolled the mask down over his face, and lifted his window. In the sill, gathered in the corner, was a teaspoon of dirt, enough to fill a board game hourglass. Just like the bit he saw while waiting to see Dean Kushner. This time, he leaned in and blew it away, the grains of it dispersing into the air. Then, thinking nothing of it, he climbed out his dorm room window into the night.

The moon was a lightbulb dangling from a high ceiling. But in Brooklyn, there were no stars. Not in the sky. Miles, climbed alongside his building up to the roof. Once there, he looked out at the New York City skyline and imagined that all the stars that were supposed to be there had fallen, and now sparkled much closer to the ground.

He took a deep breath in, and as he exhaled, he jumped.

AIR

When I'm in
the air
I feel

free. Like something
someone
has

let go of.
A kite whose string
has slipped

from a palm.
Or a dollar
that has

fallen from a pocket
in the fall.
I feel

like there's something
I can maybe
let go of,

too. I feel
like I can
let go.

Miles let himself fall for a few moments before finally shooting his web, connecting it to the corner of another building, and swinging to its rooftop. From there, he ran and jumped roof to roof as if they were concrete lily pads. Jumping and leaping, leaping and jumping across the borough until he got to the Brooklyn Bridge, where he used his web to climb up onto the cables and ran up the steel rope and back down it like the most impressive high-wire walker ever. So fast, no one saw him. And if they did, well . . . it's New York.

After the bridge, Miles went back to roof hopping until he finally made it to the wishing well of weird, the cesspool of filament and filler and fun, the tourist trap of all tourist traps, Times Square.

Even the name describes the experience. If you spend two hours there, it'll feel like four.

TIMES SQUARE

I haven't been here since
me and Ganke came to meet a kid
from the Bronx he was supposed
to swap sneakers with.

Even trade. Equal value.
Head nod, hand off.
A pair of Dunks for the kid.
A pair of snow gloves for Ganke.

After he calmed down, Ganke
insisted on putting the gloves on,
turning his hands to childproof
bear paws. And as we walked

down 42nd Street toward
the train, we laughed hysterically
at how difficult it suddenly was
for him to flip a bird.

Before that time, Miles had been to Times Square another time with his uncle Aaron. Uncle Aaron had taken Miles with him to show him the New York that Miles had seen only on TV his whole life.

"Brooklyn is yours, but this could be yours, too," his uncle said, arms outstretched. But Miles looked around, confused.

"The lights or the office buildings?" he asked.

Uncle Aaron laughed. "The excitement. That's all I ever wanted, kid. To live a life worthy of the lights." Uncle Aaron looked up at the flashing billboards. A pop star with purple hair blew a kiss.

"And how you planning to do that?" Miles asked.

Uncle Aaron cut his eyes at Miles. "Shit, me and your father were supposed to be famous crooks until he went legit, and I . . . well, let's just say the lights are still calling my name." The digital image of the purple-haired pop star changed to another advertisement. This one was for a tech company: OSBORN Industries.

THIS TIME

I walk
through the
crowd

like clouds
of local
skateboarders
and scammers
and visitors
who got
no idea

they just
speedbumps
in the way
of things.

Who got
no idea
as they take
pictures of
people in
costumes
that they
in costume, too.

Costumes
that scream:

Draw me
with a big head
and sell me
a stale churro,

49

or a frank in
puddle water,
or a CD of
your rap group
even though no
one listens to
CDs no more.
But, hey, it's a
souvenir of
that one time
you were in
Times Square
pretending to
be famous,
looking for
famous people
in the Big Apple,

happy to
be amongst
the worms
that wake up late
because they
know you
are always
on time.

—————

Miles swam through the buzzing crowd. The basketball teams selling candy, the candy sellers selling the fact that they weren't pretending to be on basketball teams, the break-dancers and skateboarders. Miles was almost sideswiped, not by either of them but by a woman holding a sign that said, CENSORSHIP IS THE CHILD OF FEAR AND THE FATHER OF IGNORANCE.

50

Miles studied the sign for so long it got weird for the lady.

"What?" she asked, shifting in her skin.

"Oh, sorry . . . nothing," Miles said, realizing he was probably freaking her out. "I was just wondering who ignorance's mother is?"

Miles was being serious, but the lady smiled, clearly amused by his question. Moments later, before Miles could ask another amusing question, an older man with a child tapped Miles on the shoulder.

"Can I get a photo with my grandson?" the man asked, pulling his wallet from his back pocket.

"Um . . ." Miles glanced at the sign lady. She shrugged, urged him to do it.

"Please," the man said, stuffing a ten-dollar bill in Miles's hand. His grandson sidled up next to Miles and posed. Flashed a snaggle-toothed cheese. Unsure of what to do, Miles smiled behind his mask. "Thanks," the man said.

And then came another. And another. Each time Miles reluctantly receiving payment. Finally, after the fifth or sixth photo, there was another tap on his shoulder. It was . . . Spider-Man. At least, someone *pretending* to be Spider-Man.

"Dude, what are you doing? We don't cannibalize!" Pretend Spidey snapped.

"What you talkin' 'bout?"

"This is my corner. Find another one to work. I'm trying to make money, but I can't because your costume looks . . . brand-new." Pretend Spider-Man pinched and tugged at the material serving as Miles's second skin. "And it fits way better. You're making it hard for me, bro. Please, cut me some slack. I got bills to pay, too, y'know?"

Miles nodded, mumbled under his breath, "This ain't no costume. It's a uniform." Then moved on.

PICKPOCKET

It ain't an easy thing
to notice and usually

looks like a bump, just
a bump, no different

than any other bump
on a busy boulevard,

one met by a *Pardon me* or
a *Watch where you goin'.*

But if you from here and
got some sense, you know

a bump can be because a
back pocket is a bull's-eye.

———————

It happened so fast.

Miles had been trying to find a different place to stand, not to take pictures (though he did like doing that) but to sit and watch people be . . . people, when suddenly his spidey-sense tingled. He quickly turned around, only to be met by a young guy with his hands up, trying to slide by him.

"Just trying to get by," the man said. But Miles continued to watch the guy as he snaked through the crowd past the old man selling pretzels, the young woman selling sweet cashews and walnuts, and the various (other) weirdos dressed as superheroes. Miles followed behind, craning his neck to keep an eye on the guy, when finally, the snake bumped an older man in front of him. The same man who asked Miles for a photo. The one with the cute grandson. Miles saw the wallet be plucked from the back pocket of the old man, watched it all happen so effortlessly, so swiftly, that if he wasn't looking for it, he might've missed it. But Miles didn't.

"Hey!" Miles yelled. The thief looked over his shoulder, saw Miles, but tried to play cool. To him, this was just another 42nd Street odd-ball in a costume. But when Miles leapt over the twenty or thirty people between them, it became clear Miles was the real thing.

The thief darted through the busy throng. And Miles chased behind him, but not before he grabbed the old man's shoulder.

"Wait for me," Miles said. The old man had no clue what was going on, but he watched as Miles zipped through the mass, unable to get a clear shot from the street to fire his web. So he shot it up in the air, splat it to a traffic light, and swung just barely above the crowd's heads, flinging himself forward, landing square on the thief's back. They rolled and bowled over a few bystanders before Miles grabbed the pickpocket by his collar.

"Please don't make this worse," Miles warned. "Just give it to me."

"Get off me, freak!" The crook thrashed around under Miles's weight.

"I've had such a long day. Seriously. I just came out for some fresh air," Miles said calmly. Then he raised his fist. "Please."

"Okay, okay." The thief gave in. Gave up. Handed Miles the wallet, both afraid and annoyed. Miles took a five-dollar bill he'd received from one of the tourists for a photo and stuffed it in the young dude's pocket. The opposite of pickpocketing. The wallet, however, went back to its owner, who'd been anxiously awaiting Miles's return.

MORE AIR

Back up
in the air.

Clapping coming
from beneath

the stars.
Back in

my room,
reminded again,

I am not a
villain.

No matter
what they say.

No matter
what they teach,

nothing should
be stolen.

Not a wallet
nor a wish.

———————

Back at his building, Miles eased into the window, being extra care-
ful not to wake Ganke, even though there was nothing he could *actually* do to wake Ganke.

REM

I learned about REM sleep
last year in biology class, how there
are steps to sleep, how every night
we gotta journey up some hill
while lying down, three stages
until landing on REM.

Means *Rapid Eye Movement*
and it's where the healing happens,
where the body licks its wounds,
prepares itself for the war of every day,
the boring banging against a humdrum,
school pulling muscles and breaking bones.

If I listen closely, close close, I can hear
this old building settle under
Ganke's snore, and the night snuggle under
a blanket of star and moon and ease
into its own REM.

I wonder if it, too, heals itself,
to prepare itself for the war of day.
If its eyes are flitting under their lids.
Wouldn't it be nice to know
I am something's dream?

At night there was a peace to the Brooklyn Visions Academy campus. Each path was lit by a streetlamp every thirty feet, creating a romantic walkway for no one to walk on. The moon reflected in the quad fountain like the biggest coin tossed into the wishing well no one ever wished on. And the volume of the campus lowered until nothing was heard but the faint hum of the maintenance men, beautifying what knuckleheads had sullied, and the less faint hum of Ganke breathing thunder through his nose.

DREAM

My mother always says
her mother always said

when you dream of
losing teeth, it's because

you've lost someone or
something, like the end

of a relationship or job.
But I ain't really got a job.

And my friends ain't the
kind of friends that bite.

Plus I ain't lose no teeth
in my dream. No, instead, in

my dream all my teeth had
gone chompless and spongy,

soft, like chewing on
thirty-two pieces of gum.

———————

The next morning, Miles woke up,   exhausted.
And itchy.
Skin and eyes on fire.

A.M.

Morning is always a slow go.
This morning slower as I wash,

scrub myself clean of whatever
invisible thing is raking sandpaper
across my skin, sanding me down,
shaving off layers of comfort. Let
the water from the showerhead
laser my eyes, power wash them
free of blur and red. Even make
my washcloth a makeshift pipe
cleaner, twist it into my nostrils,
spin it around up there to get
whatever is pricking me into a
storm of sneeze. And after that,

I get out and brush everything—teeth, hair,
lint from my clothes, *little* from wherever
it tends to stick on me and find my *big*
wherever it tends to hide in me.

Find the light that lifts my chin.
Find the light that lifts my chin.

With the itching and sneezing eventually subsiding, the puff of his eyes deflating by the minute, Miles reached in the back pocket of the pants that lay on the floor beside his bed, the ones he'd worn the day before, and slid a folded piece of paper from it. It was Alicia's poem. The response to the one he'd written for her:

YES, IT'S SANDALWOOD. AND . . .

You don't think I see you, hiding in the window looking
at me, looking at you, looking for some sense in poetry;
But don't you know, poetry isn't the prize, it's the prelude.

TO SNIFF A POEM

Alicia wears this perfume
that makes a home on
everything it hovers around.

Because of her, my nose
has become the neighborhood
of my dreams.

———————

Miles slid the poem into the middle of the spider book. Rereading it caused the corners of his mouth to turn up, but only for a second before remembering what the day had in store.

The rule was, whenever anyone had to go to In-School Suspension, it was required they dress up. Wear a shirt and tie. No T-shirts. No sweat-shirts. No comfort. And if anything was out of place—knot too loose, shirt wrinkled or untucked, buttons undone—you had to repeat the day. So Miles took his time and made sure his tie was tied right, but when he went through the process of buttoning every button on his button-up, including the ones on his button-down collar, he realized he'd lost a button on one of his cuffs.

"You gotta be kidding me," Miles muttered.

"What? You still got the itchies?" Ganke asked, brushing his chin with a dry toothbrush because he'd heard it activated hair follicles and would help him grow a beard. The television was on, and Ganke was staring at a commercial for an exterminator.

If you see one, there are one thousand more. Don't let pests become your chore! Call 1-800-ALL-GONE, and we'll help you get rid of those extra room-mates!

"You know that's Mrs. Tripley's husband?" he said about the old man on the TV. "I bet you she got the itchies even worse than you."

"I ain't got the itchies. That was just . . . I don't know what that was."

"Then what's wrong now?" Ganke turned the TV off, used the brush to scratch his arm.

"I'm missing a button."

"So? Just roll your sleeve."

"I can't. Not today." Miles palmed his face.

"You know how to sew?" he then asked Ganke.

"Of course," Ganke said, smirking. "I just did it. Here it goes again. *So.*"

"I'm not playing. I have to do something about this. I don't even know where the button is."

While Miles panicked, searching for the lost button, Ganke calmly set his beard brush on his desk, got down on the floor, and swiped one of Miles's web-shooters from under the bed.

"Here," he said. "Use this."

It took Miles a few seconds to realize what Ganke was telling him to do, which was to strap the shooter to his wrist and shoot web through the buttonhole, sticking one end of the cuff to the other, closing it as if there were a button there.

And once the cuff was fastened and Miles went to unlatch the web-shooter, Ganke stopped him.

"Better keep it on," he said, tucking it under Miles's other cuff. "In case that cuff comes loose again."

SPIDER FACT

Whenever a spider moves, of the eight legs, four are
always on the ground, and four are always off the ground.
Even with eight legs, it's best to not be caught flat-footed.

Best to always be prepared.

RM 501:
IN-SCHOOL SUSPENSION

HOW IT WORKS

A packet:
worksheets from
every class.

One classroom.
One proctor.
One guard.

Lessons,
like being
incarcerated
and receiving
letters from family

who've written
to say
they love you
in a code
you ain't

never learned
to crack,

and expect you
to write back.

———————————

"Brooklyn Visions Academy prides itself on being a progressive school, working to help raise brilliant, self-aware citizens through rigorous curriculum, ample space for healthy and challenging social interaction, and even a thoughtful disciplinary system, where if a scholar has made an infraction and is required to attend In-School Suspension, that scholar will be provided with work by their teachers, but that work will be tailored to thinking about personal responsibility" is what Dean Kushner told Miles's parents when they were touring the school when he'd first been admitted. Then, the dean, with a constipated smile, added,

"Can't have our scholars being scumbags."

THE PLEDGE   OF ANNOYANCE

I pledge allegiance to the Flag
    and to these feet which I do drag.
And to the Republic for which it stands
    on my last nerve and my two hands.
With liberty and justice for all,
    suspended for not playing small.

How did Miles feel about being in suspension? Well, let's just say he was . . . annoyed.

"Welcome to In-School Suspension," Coach Holt, the proctor said, after the pledge, as if the ISS room was a welcoming place. This room was straight from a page of an old book, everything aged and wooden. The desks were made of wood. The chairs, too. As if splinters and achy backs were the goal. Discipline through discomfort. Miles and his fellow attendees took their seats, after, of course, a thorough ISS dress code check from the guard, who only referred to Miles as *Big Man.*

"Collar check, Big Man." Miles lifted his chin.

"Tie check, Big Man." The guard wiggled Miles's knot.

"Cuff check, Big Man." Miles hesitated, but extended his arms. Thankfully, the web was holding up.

And on and on.

Once the inspection was done, Miles took a seat closer to the front.

"State your names," the guard commanded, and each student obliged.

"Miles Morales." *Not Big Man.*

"Brad Canby."

"Alicia Carson."

"Tobin E. Rogers."

"*E.?*" Brad blurted. "*E.?* Come on. You not an attorney, you in high school. And if you were an attorney, you'd clearly be a terrible one because, well, you couldn't even get *yourself* out of trouble!"

Coach Holt ignored Brad's joke and began handing out the day's packets as the morning announcements played over the intercom.

"Yesterday, the girls' soccer team won in a close match over St. Stephen's." Dawn Leary's voice popped over the speakers. "Madison Trent scored two goals in the final minutes, securing the victory." The announcements went on. Boys' soccer ended in a draw. Then boys' basketball.

"Unfortunately, the losing streak continues," Dawn said. Coach Holt sat down at a claw-foot desk at the front of the class, which was the coolest piece of furniture in the ISS room. That and the unnecessary globe ornamenting it. The same could *not* be said, however, for the cheesy poster taped to the board behind her of the word RESPONSIBILITY, each letter filled in with a swatch of the New York City subway map. An unfortunate design choice.

"Good luck next time, boys," Dawn said. Coach Holt shook her head and sulked. "This concludes our morning announcements. Have a good day, BVA, and remember, vision is at the center of all we do."

PROCTOR: COACH HOLT

Proctor is a funny word.

So close to *doctor*, except a doctor
supposed to help us while a
proctor's job is to simply watch us

die, while slowly dying with us.

Whenever Coach Holt wasn't in Room 501 babysitting the students who ended up in ISS, she coached the boys' basketball team. Neither job was all that fun, and she only took one of them seriously. That being said, she was much nicer than she looked (her hair was moussed into a helmet, and she spoke out the side of her mouth as if it were half-zipped), and she also understood that most young people just needed a little coaching.

Only problem was she wasn't that good at coaching.

CELLMATE No. 1: ALICIA CARSON

She got this way of moving
like she's magnetized by the world,
like she's being yanked toward
whatever life is meant for her.

An express train of expression,
on track but way off the tracks.
Far from Harlem but got graffiti
poems in the grooves of her palms.

And everybody try to make her
out to be vandalism, like her being
here defaces the facade until
parents like mine come visit

to see if their child will attend
this grand opportunity. Then
Alicia is seen less like a blotch
and more like a billboard.

Five days ago—last Thursday—Alicia was sitting in that very room, for the exact reason she was sitting in that room now. For telling Mr. Chamberlain who she was, and who she wasn't.

> Who she was: a person.
> Who she wasn't: a pincushion, punching bag, puppet . . .
> You know the rest.

CELLMATE No. 2: BRAD CANBY

Everything is a joke, a game to him, a comma in an unending,
    unstoppable sentence
that will continue to roll on because his daddy donates more than
    donuts to the parent-teacher
meetings, and so Brad gets to be a no treated like a yes.

———————————

Brad was a jerk. But mainly to teachers. The kid was allergic to authority.

Also, when they all arrived in the ISS room—Miles arriving first— Brad asked Miles to move out of his seat. Not in a mean way, but in a *this has just always been my seat* way.

Yes, Brad had his own seat in suspension, which might seem like he's a *yes* treated more like a *no*. But if he weren't a Canby, if he were treated like any other student, there would be no question of whether he was a *no* or a *yes*, or even a *maybe*. He would be . . . a goner.

Also, Brad was on the basketball team. The losing basketball team. Which meant Coach Holt was his coach. So even suspension wasn't really suspension for him.

But to his credit, despite all this, he did stand with Miles against Mr. Chamberlain, which was the reason he was in ISS this time. Kept the chant going even after Miles had left the room. And even though he loved trouble anyway . . . *that* was cool.

CELLMATE No. 3: TOBIN E. ROGERS

I'd never really paid any attention to him,
but any teenager who uses their middle initial
is probably worth paying attention to.

————————

Miles wasn't sure what Tobin was doing in ISS, but he knew he hadn't gotten in trouble for the same things he, Alicia, and Brad had because Tobin wasn't in Mr. Chamberlain's class. He didn't even look like he could do anything to get him in this kind of trouble. Not to mention, he worked in the library. And on top of that, was the librarian's pet.

But then again, Miles didn't look like he could do anything to get in this kind of trouble either.

CELLMATE No. 4
GUARD: BREWTON

Had no problem
standing with his arms pretzeled
and his chest all swole up
and his neck all veiny
like he ate middle fingers
every meal but never could quite
swallow them down, so they just
lodged right there in his esophagus
and could come up at any moment
and spew onto any of us.

———————————

Brewton, or Officer Brewton, or Mr. Security Guard, or Uniform Too Tight, or World History Globe Head, or whatever else students at the school could come up with whenever they saw him, was the guard who monitored the ISS room. He had a special uniform and spent most of the day with earbuds in, blasting music, sometimes even forgetting people could hear him singing aloud. Other times not caring that people could hear him singing aloud.

The rumor was Brewton used to go to Brooklyn Visions Academy and spent so much time in ISS that when he graduated, they offered him a job. The issue with that rumor is it assumes he graduated.

CELLMATE No. 4

And

of f- course

me.

Miles adjusted himself in his seat, shimmied the knot to loosen his tie *just* enough to not be in violation. And flipped to the first page of his packet.

CELLMATE No. 5

Oh, and whatever

monster

lives in the walls.

This was a running joke. Something everyone at Brooklyn Visions Academy laughed about because every now and then there would be a clanging coming through the walls. Or a knocking. Or both. Usually both. It was similar to what the radiator sounded like in Miles's apartment when the heat was first turned on for the winter. And so the assumption was that behind the walls of the school, the old pipes were doing what old pipes do.

And kids did what kids do. Crack jokes. About anything.
And pretend something is what it ain't.

CALCULUS

FUNNY MATH

The math work might be what I
fear most because nothing be
seeming to add up for me lately,

and to add letters to the mix,
to try to convince me it's possible
that x multiplied by 4 could equal

anything other than a mess makes
me more uncomfortable than trying
to convince me—just a number

in this school—that I can be multiplied
by letters. Even if those letters make words.
And even if those words make sense.

———————

Mr. Borem—Miles's calculus teacher—had assigned a worksheet
with the following instructions attached:

*Look at these photos. Each image is different, but all take on a similar shape
and pattern created by nature. This is due to hidden equations that exist
around us. Equations that are natural parts of our lives.*

PATTERNS:

An overhead view of
rivers and tributaries running into
a larger body.

A hundred-year-old
tree with limbs corkscrewing
like Abuela's arthritic fingers.

A bolt of lightning
scattered across the dark,
turning the sky to cracked glass.

———————————

Mr. Borem's instructions (cont.):

What equations are responsible for who you are in this moment?
What patterns seem to be natural to your life?

PROBLEM

I can't think
       of nothing.
Also, I don't think
       it's fair
for him to try to
       grade me
on how well
       I can
turn my life into
       a problem.

Miles mined his thoughts. Racked his brain. Sucked his teeth.

Jotted some things.

EQUATION No. 1

$i(\text{Brooklyn}) = xo$

EQUATION No. 2

i(Visions) = I

EQUATION No. 3

I(Academy) = y?

EQUATION No. 4

$i + \text{Mr. Chamberlain's Crap} = \tfrac{1}{2}i.$

Okay, so that one Miles didn't write down. Kept that one in his head.

UGH

Why should anyone
have to take math
first thing in the morning?

If the brain could do numbers

this early in the day,
people my age wouldn't be late
to class all the time.

Miles was over math, even though it was one of those rare times
math *wasn't* actually about numbers, but instead was about equating
calculus to life. But after a few tries, Miles wasn't sure he was a good
equat-er. Or maybe he felt like *the* equator. Like some kind of divid-
ing line, always under fire. And there was no equation for that.

I LOOK AROUND THE ROOM TO GAUGE EVERYONE ELSE'S BEGINNING OF THE LONGEST DAY OF OUR LIVES

Alicia is behind me, biting the nail
of her ring finger. Her other hand
twirls one of her braids. And I try not
to stare even though I owe her a thank
you or whatever else I can think of,
because she only in here for having
my back. And I ain't saying she gotta be
no ride-or-die. She too smart for that. Even
got extra books stacked at the edge
of her desk. But still. Her tough is
touching. Got a way of making me feel.

Tobin is next to me, organizing his desk
like he setting a beautiful table
for a nasty nasty meal. His pencil
is the salad fork. His pen, the main.
A highlighter his knife. His notebook
his plate. The worksheet for whatever
his first period class was placed gently
on top. He rearranged this many times.
Made the pencil the knife. Made the pen
the salad fork. But there was no cup.
This was gonna be a dry meal.

Brad is almost asleep. Already.
Ten minutes into the day and he's ripped
the worksheet from the staple, folded it,
unfolded it, then flipped it upside down,
and has not even bothered to look at it.
He don't even try. He don't even have to.
Instead, he lazily scribbles on the back
of the paper something I knew weren't words.

This was a picture. Knowing Brad, something
silly: anatomy, a comic strip involving
anatomy (ahem), a self-portrait, perhaps.

———————————————

And Miles. Looking. At them.

SPIDER FACT

It's said
that nobody
is ever more
than ten feet
from a spider.

They be everywhere
you and me are.

And they see
everything you and me
don't. Eight-eyed view
makes for life
in panorama,

sights on what's in front
and beside and behind.

WHICH MAKES ME THINK

It's never said
just how many
feet we are from all
the other feet of
all the other skittering
and scattering things.

Not to mention their eyes.
Not to mention their teeth.

Bzzz!

Miles's spidey-sense went off, and his reflex caused him to slap his own arm, where an ant had been crawling. Spidey-sense over an ant? He'd never had that happen before.

"Eyes on your paper, Miles," Coach Holt said. She pulled a newspaper from the gym bag she always kept with her.

Brewton snatched an earbud from one of his ears and perked up like a dog that thought it heard something in another room. Or as if Coach Holt was going to roll that paper into a tight tube and throw it, tell him to fetch. And as Brewton realized there was nothing to bark at, Miles, who actually wasn't quite as sure, plucked the dead ant from his arm.

FAMILY PATTERN

Eyes on my paper.
Patterns. Patterns.

Thinking of my cousin.
Patterns. Patterns.

Thinking of my father.
Patterns. Patterns.

What about my uncle?
Patterns. Patterns.

The concept of patterns was a stressful one for Miles only because it wasn't something he hadn't already thought about. If trees and lightning and rivers could all bend and take on the exact same shapes in nature, then why couldn't he take on the same shape as his father and cousin and uncle? Miles's father turned his back on his brother, Uncle Aaron couldn't turn his back on the street, and Austin's back was against the wall. So what patterns were in Miles's future? Whatever shapes "criminals" come in? The shape of fear? The shape of hole? The shape of back?

Frustrated, Miles lifted his eyes, stared ahead at the board knowing there were no answers there. Just soft remnants of erased lessons. Ghosts from previous times.

MAPS

I notice the subway map is made
up of a similar pattern as the other
images—
         the river, the tree, the lightning.

But the difference is there's nothing
natural about a subway train. It wasn't
formed by some freak organic coincidence,
but instead by men who were willing to

dig deep to get where they were going.

———————

Miles stared at the poster, RESPONSIBILITY, and thought about
another time he'd seen a similar pattern.

A FEW YEARS AGO, JUST AFTER THE BITE, MY FOLKS TOOK ME ON A BUS TRIP TO DC
or A SUMMER VACATION WE COULD AFFORD: AN ARGUMENT

My mother told my father Washington, DC, is *not* Loíza.

My father told my mother to pack sancocho in a thermos for the journey.

My mother told my father he'd never have another spoonful until it came from Abuela's pot on the island.

My father told my mother we would go the following summer, but this summer he said I needed to see the Dr. King memorial.

My mother told my father, in that case, Ganke was coming on every trip with us until we made our way to her paradise.

My father told my mother that was mean and that she knows he loves Ganke, but also that Ganke gets on his very last nerve.

My mother told my father this was the kind of selflessness Dr. King dreamt of. And Jesucristo.

My father told my mother nothing and just pulled out a road map to see the travel route for a vehicle he wouldn't even be driving.

My mother told my father nothing and pulled out her best *think I'm playin'* face.

Ganke wondered if we'd ever go to Disney World.
I wondered why we'd ever leave Brooklyn.

Miles thought about that trip and how his father kept pulling out the map to show him the route from New York to DC, which was basically a straight line. One highway. But the map itself was far more interesting than that because it showed the way to get anywhere. This line darting out from that one. That squiggle connecting to this zigzag. It was a jumble of possibilities.

But none of those possibilities mattered to Miles's father, who was set on showing his son the MLK Memorial in Washington, DC.

"'Darkness cannot drive out darkness; only light can do that,'" he said, cutting his eyes at his wife. "Gotta be that light. And if you can't *be* it, *find* it, and it'll lift your chin. No looking down. Ever."

"I just don't know why we have to see it when I've studied him every year in school, and you make me listen to his speeches every year on his birthday, *and* my birthday, which is weird."

"*So* weird," Miles's mother chimed in, lighting the stove. It ticked, ticked, ticked before flaming on.

Miles's father set the map on the table. "Because where else in this country can you go and see a Black man's face that big? Huh?" Then Miles's father folded his arms. "And he standing like this. Like me right now. Like a pissed-off dad. When you ever seen that?"

"I see it all the time."

"But not carved into a giant stone!"

THE LAST TIME I FELT LIKE THIS I WAS ON THAT BUS

Me and Ganke board the bus, sit all the way
in the back, which is what we do when we want
to feel like we not being clocked by the adults,
            the bag lady and the map man,

never thinking about why most adults don't want
to sit in the back of the bus. I'd always assumed it
was just another one of my father's hang-ups about
            Rosa Parks Rosa Parks Rosa Parks,

but that day I realize it's because the back is where
the toilet is, and I can tell you the smell of a bus
bathroom, the door swinging open, fanning *hell nah*
            is worth fighting to keep away from.

———————————

"Miles?"

Miles stared at the board, screwed his face imagining that bus trip.
The stench of it somehow making its way to his taste buds.

"Miles?" Coach Holt repeated. "Everything all right?"

"Just thinking," Miles said, snapping out of it. Coach Holt nodded,
then pointed to his desk, nudged him with her eyes to return to the
assignment. Again.

Less thinking. More work.

ANYWAY

What equations
are responsible for
    who I am
    in this moment?

What patterns
seem to be
    natural
    to my life?

Why people always
asking me
    questions
    like this?

———————

Back to thought mining and brain racking, when—

FIRE DRILL

DRILL

Nobody ever assumes it's a fire
because the first thing teachers tell us

is not to run, proving this is planned.

Proving this is practice for the real thing
in the same way calculus is practice

for nothing. Don't take being a mathematician

to notice I never seen no one walk out a burning
building. Don't take a complex equation

to know not to flirt with flames.

—————

"Everyone, please move calmly toward the door," Coach Holt said as the fire alarm blared. She stood, patted her pockets for cell phone and keys, as Miles and everyone else in the room got up from their desks, trying to hide their excitement. It was halfway through first period of suspension, and they were already leaving the room. "Please don't run, and please stay together. Fifteen minutes, then we're right back to work."

Coach Holt did a head count as if she couldn't eyeball how many people were there.

Brewton repeated everything she said and did, but in a series of grunts.

HALLWAY

The hallway is full of
hairstyles and ill-fitted outfits:

Gunked-up spikes
and bunned-up braids.

Ponytails sprouting from the tops
of heads like fountains.

Cornrows that look like zippers
to unzip and witness slivers
of a Black kid's brain.

Buzzcuts and pixies and
still-wet whatevers.

Saggy-butt baggy jeans.
Saggy-butt skinny jeans.
Saggy-butt sweatpants.

And boots that look like bear feet,
and bare feet that secretly look like boots,

steel-toed and rugged from being stuffed
in sneakers way too small but way too fly
to not strut around in, and,

if you ask me,
way too fly to be wearing here.

Everyone was outside, gathered in the quad, teenagering. Which meant roasting and razzing. Snarking and snarling. Winnie Stockton was pretending to slap-box Ryan Ratcliffe. Chrissy Bentley was diligently working to perfect her ponytail. The triplets, Sandy, Mandy, and Brandy, gravitated toward one another, like they all had some kind of sister sonar. Judge sat on the lip of the fountain, cuffing his pants, trying to nail the scrunch-to-sneaker ratio.

And Ganke headed straight for Miles.

ALONG CAME GANKE (first five minutes)

Brewton saw him coming. Like
he knew he was coming.
And when Ganke opened his mouth,
Brewton turned his palms
into stop signs.

Turned his fingers
into fences, like
my name don't even deserve
to live in the air. Like
to call out for me is criminal.

"Don't do it, Ganke," Brewton barked. "No talking to ISS kids."

Ganke froze in his tracks. Closed his mouth. Looked at me and Alicia and Brad and Tobin lined up like figurines on a mantel. And smirked.

"Okay, Brewton. Well . . . can I talk to *you*?" Ganke asked.

Miles already knew where this was going. Actually, everyone did. Ganke was known for being silly, and when it came to Brewton, it was almost impossible for him to resist.

"Ganke, not right now."

"I just have some questions."

Brewton shook his head, waved his arms, swelled his chest. "What?"

"I just want to know, when you were born, what number were you in the litter?"

If Alicia had been drinking anything, it would've been all over the place. She spat air everywhere. Brad became a bug. Well, not really, but his eyes looked like the beginning of a bug-like transformation. Tobin giggled. And Miles just dropped his head.

Brewton narrowed his eyes into threat.

"Let me guess." Ganke wound up. "You were the runt, right?"

MORE JOKES FROM GANKE

Then he asks Brewton
if he's gotten used to life
on Earth and if his planet
had private schools.

Then he asks Brewton
if his head is so damn
big because his uniform
is so damn tight.

Then he asks Brewton
if he ever plans on
having kids of his own.
Then begs him not to.

———————————

By this point, Miles was laughing right along with everyone else. No one was even trying to hold it in. Except for Brewton. He looked like he wanted to wrap his hands around Ganke's neck, but he couldn't. So instead it looked like each joke had wrapped itself around his neck and was making his head even *bigger*. Explosion was near. And Coach Holt knew this, so she put a stop to Ganke's shenanigans.

"That's enough, Ganke," she said. "Unless you want to pull up a seat next to your buddy Miles here."

Ganke quieted down. Took a bow. Backed away while winking at Miles. But by then, Miles was too busy clocking Mrs. Tripley, who was walking across the quad.

TRIPLEY ON THE MOVE (second five minutes)

Mrs. Tripley usually walks around
like she lives in the books she loans.

The fairy tales and adventure stories
where she knows the happy ending

is inevitable, so frowns are futile
and should stay far, far away.

But for some reason, when she
looked toward us, the suspended,

her face fell. Sagged and drooped
like the bellies of the old men on my block.

But theirs came from beer. Hers was a plot
twist. A blow. Out the blue.

———————————

Mrs. Tripley didn't stop. She just kept walking toward the library.

And then:

FIGHT!

I didn't see it.
I didn't even hear it.

Just felt the crowd
begin to simmer,
then sizzle, then
boil and burst open.

Something was moving
everybody around.
Something was turning
all us kernels into
fake-flavored popcorn,

and there were two
questions:
Where was
the movie?
And who
were its actors?

———————

Winston Faulk vs. Brock Hanky.

Pandemonium.

PEOPLE FIGHT

People be
talking about
private school
kids like
they ain't
got hands
and feet.

———————

And like with most fights, everyone ran toward the action. Pushed and scrambled, clawing their way into the melee. Including teachers and guards, like Brewton, who were trying to break it up. And in the midst of the dust-up and confusion—people rushing past the ISS kids, bumping them—Miles eased away from the group. And when he knew it was safe, when he knew no one was paying any attention to him, he vanished. Camouflaged to separate himself from the crowd.

Miles ghosted toward the library, and as he got close, he heard Mrs. Tripley talking to herself while sweeping the walkway leading up to the library door. Miles checked his surroundings, and when he was sure he was safe, he reappeared.

"I just don't understand why he would do such a thing," she mumbled. "What could've possibly gotten into him?"

"Who?" Miles asked, worried she was talking about him. "Did what?"

DISAPPOINTMENT

Mrs. Tripley is one
of those people
you never want to
let down. She's made
of good. She's shining
armor for the kids here
who look like nights
but ain't seen as heroes.

——————————

"Oh, Miles," Mrs. Tripley said, startled by Miles creeping up on her. "Aren't you supposed to be in ISS?"

"Yeah, but I just gotta ask you something real quick."

"Can it wait until tomorrow?" she asked. Miles thought for a moment. It could have. But here he was, risking more punishment, because what he needed to ask her was burning a hole in his belly.

"I promise, I'll go right back over there." Whistles were being blown as the guards and teachers tried to regain order.

"Miles, there's a lot going on right now."

"Just one question," Miles pleaded.

Mrs. Tripley looked over Miles's shoulder, saw the crowd finally settling down.

"Hurry up," she said, nodding toward the rest of the student body. The teachers had regained their students and resumed their head counts.

"You think maybe we could do a book drive for my cousin, Austin? He's locked up in—"

Bzzz!

IF A TREE FALLS

and there is no wind,
no axe,
no bucked tooth
to topple it,

is it still considered a tree,
or is it now a trap?

————————

Miles glanced to his left, and there it was, a huge tree headed right toward him and Mrs. Tripley. He dove, pushing her out the way, both of them landing in the grass as the tree just barely missed them and crashed onto the walkway. The sound of the wood clattering on the stone reverberated around the quad.

The sound wasn't enough to break up the fight, but it was enough for Coach Holt to realize she'd lost a kid, and moments later she came calling for Miles.

"Miles!" Miles had gotten up and was now helping Mrs. Tripley to her feet. "What are you doing over here? Do you want In-School Suspension again, tomorrow?"

"No, Coach Holt. I—"

"I pulled him away, Coach," Mrs. Tripley said, sticking up for Miles. "To ask him about a book. And it's a good thing I did, because he just saved me from being flattened on the cobblestone!" And before Coach Holt could say anything, Mrs. Tripley went on. "You know the etymology of *cobblestone* is interesting because it's made up of two words. The first, *cobble*, comes from—"

Coach Holt cut her off. "Okay, okay." She waved Mrs. Tripley off, glanced over at the felled tree. "I'm not the one in class. Miles, get yourself together and come on back in."

As Coach Holt walked away, Mrs. Tripley mumbled, "Works every time." Then Miles, who was trying to brush grass stains off himself, and Mrs. Tripley, who didn't even bother trying to clean up, went and looked at what was left of the jagged tree stump. It was hollow, and small insects were crawling in and through it.

"What kind of ants are those?" Miles asked, instantly queasy. They were just like the one that had been crawling on him earlier.

Mrs. Tripley squatted down to take a closer look.

"Looks like termites. Strange for them to be so active this time of year." She reached down and let one crawl onto her hand. Then, suddenly, she pinched it between two fingers, killing it. "You get back to class."

BACK TO CLASS (three minutes late)

This was only
a fifteen-minute drill and
in fifteen minutes, there were

jokes and black eyes, busted lips
and more kids in trouble and
a tree eaten from the inside

that almost cracked my spine,
almost tore me up,
almost checked me out.

———————

Miles was late. And by the time he got back to Room 501, the door
was locked.

But when Brewton opened it, Alicia and Brad clapped for Miles.
A slow clap, to begin. Then faster. And faster. And faster. Corny-
movie style.

"That's enough," Coach Holt said.

"Come on, Coach. He's basically a . . . hero," Brad said, jokey.

"Back to work, Canby!" From Brewton. "You too, Big Man."

(BACK TO) CALCULUS

UNCONCERNED

I figure Tobin
would want to know that
Mrs. Tripley is okay.

That as far as I know
she's only suffered streaks
of green across her

back, might be some
minor purpling later.
But suddenly math

seems more important
to Tobin than the
life of his mentor.

"Miles, you're late, *and* talking?" Coach Holt said, annoyed. "You're in danger of repeating this sentence tomorrow. Please act like you got some sense."

His third warning. A danger. And he needed to act like he had some sense. But the kind of sense his mama gave him, that made him want to stay in his seat. Not the kind the spider gave him, that made him want to jump out his skin.

WHAT SPIDEY-SENSE FEELS LIKE

A pot, boiling, burning,
bubbles bursting in me, rolling
over on myself, in myself, because
someone done turned the flame on high
without me hearing the tick tick tick of the stove.

———————————

It was one of Miles's many changes since he was bitten by the spider, but it was the one mutation that didn't seem all that super. Didn't seem all that different from what he'd been taught by his parents when it came to walking around their neighborhood. Where he was from—*his* Brooklyn—required the same superpower to survive.

"Always keep your antenna up for anything that feels weird," his father told him. "Head on a swivel."

"Yeah, because you need to be able to know there's static before static knows there's you," his mother followed.

Back then, it was a gut feeling. An intuition. Now, it's a *gut* feeling . . . like, Miles's stomach tumbling. His mind buzzing and all the hair standing up on his arms and neck. This is what it meant to be Spider-Man. To feel like extra legs could sprout from your abdomen, extra eyes could blossom from your head.

TEN MINUTES LATER

We only been
back to class
maybe ten minutes,
maybe not even,

and Brad Canby
look like he's
still cheering on
Winston and Brock,

or like he
still clapping
for me, now a
standing ovation,

or like he
done became
one of those
inflatable tube

monster things
outside the used
car dealership,
all hot air, wide-eyed

and awkwardly
flailing around to
advertise what even a fool
knows is a scam.

———————————

"Canby!" Brewton barked. "What's your problem?"

BRAD GOTTA GO

When you in ISS, you can't even
piss without patrol

escorting you down the hall
like you still in elementary, walking
third tile from the wall, wishing you were

line leader just so you can have a clear view
of your destination, not just the vision

of the back of somebody else's head
who you hope is going the right way, who you
hope knows where the relief is.

———————

"If you don't let me go, I'm a have to do it right here," Brad said.
"Then we all gotta suffer through the way my pee smells when I've
had coffee in the morning, which is to say, freshly brewed."

"Ugh, please let him go," Alicia moaned before letting a chuckle
slip out when she saw Brad dancing with his hands shoved between
his legs.

Miles chuckled, too.

So did Tobin.

So did Coach Holt.

But not Brewton.

HAND   OFF (*BZZZ!*)

I feel that thing again,
the sense that I'm in
danger, and as my eyes
dart and my arm twitches,
ready to do what it naturally
does whenever I feel this way

—strike or block or swipe—

I hold off, and watch this critter
like a soft yellow ellipsis, the same
that was part of hundreds hollowing
out a tree, a termite, this time,
crawling crawling crawling
across the back of my hand.

———————————

As Brewton escorted Brad out of the classroom, Miles was pre-
occupied, watching the termite for a second before flicking it off his
hand. He watched as it hit the floor, circled for a moment, before
making its way back toward him but bumping into Tobin's foot,
crawling up his sneaker, and up his pant leg.

Miles trapped his gasp.
Tobin didn't flinch.

ISS: A STUDY

In Serious . . . Stuff

Interested in Strangling Students

Identify Scheming Scammers

Idiot Salvation Stable

Ill-tempered Scrappy Squares

Imbecilic Student Scolding

———————

Miles started scribbling on the desk in faint pencil. Distraction from the work in front of him. Distraction from the weird inside him.

The last three:

I'm Seeing Signs
I'm Sensing Something
I'm   Sorta   Scared.

HOW I LEARNED TO MIND MY BUSINESS

The thing about growing up in Brooklyn is we all learn
to mind our business before we even learn to mind our manners.

It's our first job, usually given to us at the dinner table when
grown folks are talking, on the block when mad folks are yelling,

or on the train when poor folks are begging. It don't always feel good,
and it don't really pay much, but if you get the gig wrong, it'll leave you

broke. Ain't no days off. Ain't no sick days. Ain't no vacations. But the
    best
of us know that if you want be good at it, you gotta work overtime.

Miles swallowed his alarm that a termite had crawled up Tobin's leg. Figured it was best to put his eyes back on his own work.

So he did.

But he was ready to give up on the math. He was over it. If there was an equation for his life that he could agree on, it would've had to have been:

i + procrastination = happy. Or at least, happier than wasting this kind of time doing this kind of work in this kind of . . . "class."

And to make good on that equation, he reached into his backpack and pulled out *Arachnophilia: The Strange and Unbelievable World of Spiders.*

SPIDER FACT

People who fear
spiders

    usually
overestimate their
size.

———————

Miles read from his book for a moment before glancing over at Tobin
again, wondering what the termite might've been doing in there.
But then the door opened. Brewton and a much more relaxed Brad
were back from the bathroom.

Miles caught Brewton's eye.
    "You good, Big Man?" Brewton said.
    Miles said nothing.
    Just nodded and kept reading.

BELL!

BELL

When the bell finally clangs,
the muscles in my legs

do what they've been trained
to, like my kneecaps are

spring-loaded, and snap
into action at the sound

of the bell ringing *get up,*
get going, the bell ringing

inhale something other than
the back row, the bus bathroom

of this school, the bell ringing
a song of temporary freedom.

Miles slapped his book closed and, without thinking, lifted off his seat ready to catch his breath before catching himself. Then, he lowered back onto the wooden chair. Looked around. No one else had budged, not even a little. Like they were used to being suspended.

In thin air.

CHEMISTRY

GREEN BANANAS

The worksheet says "Green Bananas."

There are three questions.

The first is:

> *If you set an underripe banana, a green one,*
> *next to an overripe banana, brown and bruised,*
> *the green banana will quickly become brown and bruised.*
>
> *Why?*

———————————

Miles rearranged the packet so that the math work was, thankfully, on the bottom, and the chemistry worksheet was on top. He read it, pondered before writing:

The brown bananas emit ethylene gas, which speeds up the ripening of the green bananas. The decaying process is called enzymatic browning.

Miles liked chemistry class. Well, really he liked Mrs. Khalil and her approach to teaching chemistry. Mrs. Khalil made chemistry feel like a necessary thing to know in order to understand how life works. How the chemicals in our bodies often make us who we are. Miles could sink his teeth into this class because it helped him think about his . . . superpowers.

He hated that word, *superpowers.* As a matter of fact, Mrs. Khalil's class made him think about how, because of the genetically altered spider bite, his body had extra chemicals, not super chemicals, which meant he was *extra* human, not necessarily *super*human.

The next questions are:

When have you been a green banana?
A brown and bruised one?

These were tough questions for Miles.

He thought for a moment about the people in his life closest to him, and whether or not they were green bananas or brown bananas, and what effect they may have had on him.

Miles was used to Mrs. Khalil asking questions like *How many elements are in the periodic table, and how many of those elements are actually found in nature?*

Not questions like *Are any of your friends or family radioactive elements in your table?* Or, in this case, *Who around you is a "brown banana"?*

BANANA TREE

1. UNCLE AARON

My uncle is dead.
But when he wasn't dead,
people refused to see his life
as a life for whoever people
call good or normal or

not in suspension.

I loved him. Because
whatever was in his
walk that made him bob and
weave the wind, I got. And
whatever was in his back
that made him carry on
his carry-on, I got. And
whatever was in his throat
that kept his voice from
rippling into vibrato,

I got. Now.

———————

Miles thought about his uncle. Not about the bad his uncle had
done in the streets of New York, but about who his uncle was to him.
Uncle Aaron saw himself in Miles. The him he could've been. He saw
Miles as a better future, far from the one he and his brother—Miles's
father—ever had. Even far from the one Austin had now.

2. AUSTIN

My whole life, everybody been saying
the same thing about books, but not
when they talking about books, but
when they talking about people

don't nobody want to read.
They say not to judge a book
by its cover. Austin is a novel.
Each chapter building on the

next. Exposition. Rising action.
Conflict. A hero's journey. But
covers do what covers are meant
to do. They cover. Protect. Keep

the pages from fraying. From
being damaged by bad weather
like storms or the sticky and oil
of foreign fingers who like to

thumb through a story, skim
for a scheme or an explosion
all for the sake of entertainment
before tossing aside. What no one

cares about—too concerned with
unsavory covers—is how all these words,
all this story, hard written but barely
read, are bound to such a strong spine.

Miles had been thinking about Austin a lot. About how he was an unfinished story. A book slammed shut. A judged cover. But a sturdy spine. This was also why Miles thought about whether or not Austin and everyone else locked up with him had good books to read, and why they might've needed them. And why Miles needed Mrs. Tripley to help him get them. Stories to complement their own. Words that would bang louder in their heads than the iron gates. Paperback promises of a future or a fantasy or an unknown family member who has not forgotten them.

3. GANKE

My best friend a Korean boy
with a keen taste in sneakers
and snickering. Boy got a joke
for just about everything and
a fresh pair to match. First kid
I ever knew with a pair of 1s
from 1985. Said they were a
gift from his father, who got
them as a gift from Michael Jordan.
I know Ganke lying, but I act like
he not because I don't want him to be.
I want it to be true he was given
them special shoes straight from
the legend and got the nerve to
wear them every day just because
he think it's funny when people
look at him like he gotta be joking.

———————

Miles thought about Ganke. His homeboy. His Day One. His Ace.
Who he *usually* got in trouble with. Who he always got out of trouble
with. Who he laughed with and sometimes cried with. Ganke held all
Miles's secrets. Even his biggest one—

NOT TO MENTION

Ganke knows I'm—
and he knows I can—
and all that.

He's even seen me—
and defeat—
and all that.

Matter fact when I first—
and felt like—
he encouraged all that.

———————

Ganke was there when Miles's "super symptoms" (sticky hands and sparks of strength) started. As a matter of fact, one of the earliest moments was when Miles and Ganke boarded that bus for the trip down to DC. You know, the one Miles's father had planned. Miles's hand was still slightly swollen, and his mother, who'd assumed it was just a normal spider bite, continued to nurse it with Neosporin.

"Yo, it smells like somebody ate french fries and fruit punch for lunch and puked it all over this bus," Ganke said about the stinky bathroom. Miles laughed.

"Nah, it smell like your shoes smell when you take 'em off and spray bathroom air freshener in 'em, thinking that's gonna help!" Miles cracked. This was true. Ganke did sometimes spray air freshener in his dank sneakers.

"Nah, I got one, it smells like old Tupperware in there," Ganke said.

"But what was in the Tupperware?" Miles asked.

"It don't matter! They *all* stink!" The boys laughed and laughed, until the dust and dander caught in the fibers of the old bus seats irritated Miles's nose. He sneezed. And when he did, he disappeared. Not vanished, but just blended in with the seats, which looked like the carpets at the local skating rink.

"Oh shh—" Ganke caught himself.

"What?" Miles asked.

"Bro, you . . . I can't see you." Ganke reached out for Miles's shoulder. It was like he'd grabbed solid air.

"What you mean?" And just then, Miles sneezed again and reappeared. Ganke's eyes almost shot out of his face.

"Can you see your reflection in the window?" he asked, pointing toward the glass.

"Of course."

"Okay, so keep looking." And moments later, Miles sneezed again, causing his reflection to vanish in the glass. He yipped.

Miles's mother, recognizing the sound of her son, turned around. She flashed a concerned face, and Ganke just pointed to the bathroom door. Shrugged. His mother turned back around.

"Ganke, what am I gon' do?" Miles whispered, waiting for another sneeze.

"You gotta lock yourself in that bathroom and wait until the sneeze attack is over."

"*What?*" Miles was mortified. "The stinky bathroom? But what if I throw up in there?"

"Who knows . . . maybe you . . . disappear forever." Ganke got up from the seat and held the bathroom door open, the smell of spicy death wafting out. "So don't puke!"

142

4. MA

My mother do for me
what mothers do.

Figures out how to hear me

when I can't say
what I can't say.

Miles thought of his mother. Everything she'd given him, all she'd done to keep him seeing life as an open field to run around in. For him to find his voice and scream in. For him to feel fresh air on his face and feel like the breeze was his to bend.

5. DAD

My father do for me
what fathers do.

Figure out how to show me

how to show up
and shine.

(Find the light that lifts my chin.)

———————

Miles thought of his father. Everything he'd given him, all he'd done to keep him on the straight and narrow. And how along that straight and narrow road it was important for Miles to be grateful for, but also to question, each stone, each twig, each blade of grass.

And if there was a banana tree, Miles's father would've wanted him to question that, too.

144

6. (EVEN) HOUSE

My barber been cutting my hair
since I was a little thing. Made me
wait my turn. Sat me up in the chair
first on a phone book until I was big
enough for my head to be high enough
without one. Smocked me. Tissue around
my neck like Father Jamie's collar. Asked my father
what I was getting. My father would tell him
what my mother said I was getting. Clippers on.
Cut with the grain. Hair falling down
my face like ash with specks of snow in it
because dry scalp runs in our family. And he
would always remind me as I examined
each clipping, each swatch of what had
grown out of me naturally, that dandruff
ain't got nothing to do with dirty.

———————————

Miles considered the barbershop—because you *gotta* consider the
barbershop—and how his barber, House, and all the men who hung
out there seemed to show him different things. Who to be. Who not
to be. How to move. How not to move. How to look. How to play
chess. How to tip. How to fold bread. How to separate it for different pockets. How to fight and forgive. How to swing. How to duck.
How to clean. How to cuss. How to pose in front of a mirror like the
mirror looking at you funny. Like the mirror owe you money. The
importance of a nickname.

"Aight, Shorty Forty," House would always say whenever it was Miles's turn for a cut. He called him that because Miles always got a 4.0 on his report card. But the other folks in the shop had different names for him.

Derrick, who was always there playing chess, would say, "That's Smarty Arty."

Frankie, who was always playing against Derrick, would chime in, "You mean Baby Einstein."

Big Bird, who was a giant man who looked just like Big Bird, hated the nickname Baby Einstein—even though he didn't seem to mind the nickname Big Bird—and always made it known.

"Why just because Miles is smart we gotta name him after some old white man?"

"Einstein wasn't just any white man!" Frankie snapped.

"Shut up, Frankie. You don't even know what Einstein was known for," House said.

"Sure I do. For being smart, just like Miles," Frankie replied.

"I heard he couldn't even tie his own shoes," Mr. Branson, the neighborhood hoarder, said. He was having his fade tightened up and loved to call Miles Bug. He called *everybody* Bug. Except bugs. He called them family.

"That's why I call Miles Long Distance," Big Bird said.

"What does that even mean?" Mr. Branson said.

"Exactly. What the hell you talkin' 'bout," House said. Big Bird shook his head.

"It means he gon' go farther than y'all stupid asses." Big Bird pointed at everyone but Miles.

Fat Tony, who'd been sitting in there with his dog, waiting for his cut, spoke up. "Now, that I agree with. L'il Man gon' save the world."

7. SPIDER-MAN

Everybody so proud of me,
but not many know the me
I'm still getting to know.

The me that puts on new skin
and knits a safety net for strangers
with his bare hands

in the blink, or better yet,
the wink of an eye.

Where I exist. In the joke. The lie.
The *watch this*. The secret. The *gotcha*.
Half seen, even by me, because how
can I be a hero if I can't save myself?

Maybe part of being a hero
is believing you one. And
another part of being a hero
is never seeing yourself as one.

One eye open, one eye closed.
But who, in this mask, can tell
which is which?

Even though Miles's relationship with being Spider-Man was one he was still getting used to, he knew that trying to help people was ultimately a good thing. And even though when he put the mask on, it seemed as though the Miles part of him disappeared, he knew that wasn't true. He was just as much Miles as Spider-Man as he was as Shorty Forty or Smarty Arty or Baby Einstein. Just as much Miles as he was as Mijo.

Therefore . . .

NO

I ain't never been
no green banana.

I was born brown,
and what some call

bruises be Brooklyn
beauty marks.

Miles wrote this on his paper in response to the question. Then added,

And is it the banana's fault that it has aged this way?

COACH HOLT BLOWS HER WHISTLE

Tells us to pause.
Tells us to get up.
Tells us to stretch.

Arms out. Rotate clockwise.
Then counterclockwise.
Then arms down. Touch

our toes. Then arms up
over our heads.
Reach. Reach.

Miles glanced back at Alicia, who had reached forward while stretching, gently touching the middle of Miles's back, and was now reaching above her head, chewing on her smile, a sliver of stomach exposed, her navel almost identical to the knots in the cherry wood, winking at him.

"Y'all can say a few words to each other," Coach Holt said.

But no one uttered a syllable. Not even Miles. Not at first. But then Alicia, now arms down, said, "Is it true?"

At first Miles thought she was talking to him. But he quickly realized she wasn't. She was talking to Tobin.

"Is what true?" Tobin replied, his thick brows meeting like caterpillars kissing.

"That you in here for stealing books?" Alicia asked.

Tobin didn't answer. Just sat back down in his seat. Picked up a pencil, began tap-tap-tapping.

"*What* he do?" Brad eavesdropped.

"Yeah, what he do?" Miles followed.

"I heard he was stealing books from the library and destroying 'em," Alicia said.

"Destroying 'em?" Miles was confused.

"Yeah, they found hundreds of books under his bed. No pages. Just spines."

"You got books right in front of you," Tobin said about Alicia's stack. He stretched his neck. "Baldwin. Bambara. Baraka. Who else?"

"I checked them out a long time ago."

"So, they're overdue?" Tobin asked.

"Don't matter. I'm glad I kept them so you couldn't destroy 'em like you did the others," Alicia said.

"They had bugs in them, Alicia," Tobin said. "Poisonous ones. But no one would believe me, so I had to take care of them myself."

"So you tellin' me Tripley, a woman whose husband we all know is an exterminator—"

"I love those commercials! *If you see one, there are one thousand more!*" Brad imitated the man on the commercial. His funny voice and serious face.

"Right. And he wants us to believe she didn't believe him, and that they punished him for doing the right thing, which sounds like bull," Alicia said. To Brad. About Tobin.

"Isn't that what *you're* here for?" Tobin replied. "For doing the right thing?"

Alicia nodded, reluctantly. He had a point.

"So, Tobin E. Rogers, attorney-at-law, is basically . . . a hero, too!" Brad razzed, starting the slow clap but ending it immediately once he realized no one was with him.

Miles turned to Tobin, who forced a smile and continued tap-tap-tapping,

tap-tap-tapping,

tap-tap-tapping.

THIRTY SECONDS BEFORE SITTING

Ain't no way we can
all just sit back down after
that small taste of stand up.

Ain't no way a body gonna
be good with curling up when
it knows what it means to unfold.

Ain't no way we can go
from trees, and rivers, and bolts
of lighting, back to wrong right angles.

Ain't no way we can just weave our
selves between wood and steel and
plastic after we'd swam in a pool of air.

Ain't no way we can just trade
a serving of wassups and what-nows
for a feast of what-else and worksheets.

Ain't no way, ain't no way, ain't no way.

———————————

Miles still couldn't shake the fact that a few minutes before the Tobin
investigation, Alicia had grazed his back, pushing an imaginary
button, turning him on. He also couldn't shake the fact that Tobin,
a kid who used the middle initial in his name, the library nerd, had
been suspended for stealing and destroying library books. Seemed
like such a silly thing to do. And weird. And also sorta . . . Tobin.
Because if anyone was going to try to save the library, it would be him.

TOUCH

How do I ask
Alicia if I can return
the favor and touch
her back? Maybe not
on her back, but the palm

of her hand,
or in between her fingers
where the webbing is
to see if maybe we
stick together.

───────────

While Miles was surprised about Tobin, Brad was taking the news completely differently.

"Wait," Brad started, the dim lightbulb in his head flickering. "Tobin, you're the expert on this, so tell me . . . should I be scared to open my textbooks? I mean, they might . . . need to be destroyed, too, right?"

Brad emptied his backpack, and the bricks that double for textbooks slammed onto the floor.

"These gotta be full of bugs! Keep 'em away from me!" Brad shrieked.

And everyone howled. Except for Tobin, who didn't even acknowledge the joke. Who had already gotten back to work. Who was now erasing something on his paper, furiously scrubbing the pencil across the page, scrubbing scrubbing scrubbing.

WARNING

Brewton tells us to settle
down. Tells us all the things

we better do.

We better sit down.
We better shut up.
We better know we ain't

too good to not be back

suspended tomorrow.
And if we are, Brewton
says, it's because we ain't

know how to settle
down. So too bad.

———————

Miles sat down, cut his laughter off and stopped running his mouth
like closing off flow to a spigot.

Not a drip, or a drop.

CLANG CLANG KNOCK KNOCK

Sounds like the people behind the wall
are returning to their seats, too. Sounds
like giant chairs scraping across the floor
or being thrown around, broke apart.

Coach Holt said, "See? Don't make me let them out!" She knocked
on the wall, pretending to calm down the make-believe monsters.

ERASER

I figure
maybe it's
the embarrassment
that makes him
do it. That makes him
upside-down his pencil
and rub its eraser
until it disintegrates,
until it erases
the actual paper,
burns through it,
eats it like food.

Miles, preparing himself to get back to work, glanced over at Tobin, who had a tiny mountain of eraser shavings gathered at the corner of his desk. Miles watched as a termite, maybe the same one that climbed up his pant leg, the one that was on Miles's hand, climbed from outside Tobin's shirt, up his neck, up the side of Tobin's face, and into his ear.

What?! Miles thought, but didn't say. Instead, he whispered Tobin's name, trying to get his attention to tell him about the bug that had just made its way into his head. But Tobin didn't answer. "Tobin!" Miles whispered louder, defeating the purpose of a whisper.

"Miles!" Coach Holt sparked.

Miles zipped it. Locked it. Threw away the key.

WHAT SENSE?

Head buzzing.
Body ringing.
Vertebrae electric.
Brain throbbing.
Throat tightened.
No idea
            why.

———————————

As Miles's spidey-sense lit up the insides of his body . . . again,
as he gave the room a quick once-over to see where the danger was,
what was coming for him,

Tobin leaned over to the corner of his desk and blew the eraser shavings off.

Right in Miles's direction.

ITCH

Had I known better,
I would've pulled off
the greatest magic trick ever
and caught a thousand pieces
of rubber dust between
my fingers. But, no, I didn't
know better. So I didn't.

———————————

The dust flew into Miles's eyes. Every bit of eraser sticking to his irises as if pulled there by gravitational force. Miles hissed from the burn, threw his hands up to his face, quickly rubbing his eyes, trying to flush them out.

"What the . . . why you do that?" Miles asked. "Seriously, there were so many other places to blow that."

"Miles!" Coach Holt, again. "Come on, man. This is your last warning. I'm serious."

"He just blew eraser crap in my eyes," Miles groaned, still wiping.

"It was an accident," Tobin said. "Sorry, Miles."

"Whatever, it's fine." Miles pressed his fists against his eyes. "It's fine."

He gave his eyes a few more rubs, opening and closing them until he felt like most of the eraser ash was gone. Then he tried focusing back on his work.

But the page seemed to have become quicksand, the words now disappearing between the lines.

I BLINKED

Opened my eyes.
Then blinked again,

this time a long blink.
Squeezed my eyes

shut for a three-count.
Long enough to whisper

a three-second prayer:
Let there be light.

When Miles opened his eyes, the words written in his scratchy hand-writing had returned: *I have never been a green banana.*

He was relieved. Figured it was just irritation.

HOW TO CATCH A MOUSE (*EVERYTHING IS FINE*)

When I was little little,
like five or six or maybe even four,
but probably not four because
I don't remember four like that,

there were mice in our apartment.
Any hole in them old building walls
is enough space for the gummy bones
of rodents. And at night, when they'd

skitter around, I would trap myself
under a pillow and hum for ten seconds,
then listen. And if I heard nothing, I'd
pretend I'd heard nothing the whole time.

———————

And if it wasn't just irritation, he was willing to convince himself it
was just irritation.

BACK TO BANANAS (*FOCUS, FOCUS*)

Can't nobody do much with
no green banana, anyway.
All bitter and tough.

But when ripe, when
darkened far past the yellow,
despite its bruises, it becomes
the most nutritious.

But the thing is,
    it's only sweet for a little while.
Yeah, it's sweet only for a little while.

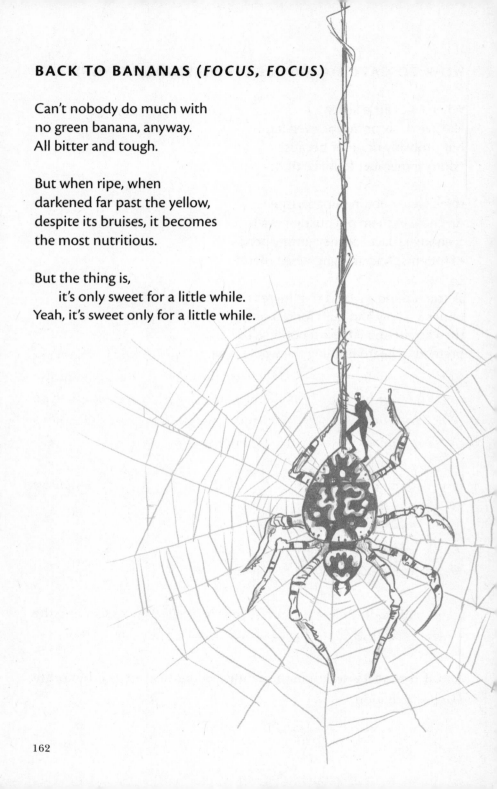

Relieved that his vision had cleared, Miles wrote this. At first he thought maybe he was taking the assignment too far. Maybe he'd get in more trouble for thinking outside the box and questioning the question. But he knew Mrs. Khalil wouldn't mind. She was the type of teacher who was open to this kind of push. Once she asked Miles's class to come up with their own theories of how life began.

How did a bunch of simple molecules meet up and combine and then replicate into complex chemical structures that formed the whole planet?

Some people said it was God.
Some people said it was the big bang.

Miles said, "I don't know, but I believe in small things changing the course of reality."

Why wouldn't he believe that? A tiny spider had changed his life forever.

ALSO ABOUT BANANAS

What does it mean to have to
strip a thing of its skin to enjoy it?

—————

And then.
The words.

They began to tremble and fade again.

Miles blinked.   Wiped his eyes. Wiped. Wiped. Wiped.   Blinked.

HOW TO KEEP A GIRLFRIEND (*EVERYTHING REALLY IS FINE*)

There was this
other time in
middle school
when I caught
my girlfriend,
Tracy North,
kissing Angelo
Something. I
don't remember
his last name.

What I do
remember is
they were at
a pizza place,
eating slices
like they were
on a date, and
Tracy said she
wasn't kissing
him to kiss him,

but to kiss me
better. And then
kissed me, first
time with tongue,
and I acted like
I hadn't tasted
pepperoni, even
though she was
eating cheese,
and cheesed.

Again, Miles tried to steady himself. Tried to shake the shaky words off. Tried to shake them straight.

Get it together. Nothing's wrong. Nothing's wrong. Get it together.

SO TO ANSWER THAT SECOND QUESTION (*FOCUS, MILES, FOCUS*)

When have you been a green banana?
　　My name is Miles Morales.
　　I attend Brooklyn Visions Academy.
　　People think I'm something else.

A brown and bruised one?
　　My name is Miles Morales.
　　I attend Brooklyn Visions Academy.
　　People think I'm something else.

———————

Maybe a lemon, Miles thought as the letters continued to quiver and pulse from seen to unseen.
Maybe a pickle.

He blinked. Reached for his spider book. Opened it to where Alicia's letter had it marked.

Took a break.

SPIDER FACT

Did you know some male spiders
give dead flies to female spiders,
gift wrapped in intricately patterned
web, humbly, hoping this will be
enough to mate and not be murdered.

Miles read the spider fact and then unfolded Alicia's note for the forty-eighth time. He wanted to see if anything had changed, or if his eyes would see the words as he'd seen them that morning, and the forty-six other times he'd read it.

YES, IT'S SANDALWOOD. AND . . .
You don't think I see you, hiding in the window looking
at me, looking at you, looking for some sense in poetry;
But don't you know, poetry isn't the prize, it's the prelude.

Perfect.

But he wasn't sure how to respond or what to say next; still, he knew he had to say something. So he took his pencil and scribbled in the page of the book, right under the spider fact:

I can offer more than a fly.
The least I can do is a slice or two.
I'm even willing to come to Harlem.

Then he tore the page from the spine slowly enough for it to be a silent act. But Tobin heard it, cut his eyes toward Miles. And smiled.

BELL!

LUNCH

AS FAR AS RIO MORALES IS CONCERNED

To my mom:

I ain't never been bullied on no other block.
I ain't never been punched in the face.
I ain't never had my pockets patted, turned out, made basset hound ears.
I ain't never had to run to keep my shoes.
I ain't never been roasted so bad my skin felt like it was actually hot
    and crispy.
I ain't never been laughed at by someone I like or betrayed by
    someone I love.
I ain't never been lied to or cheated or manipulated or misunderstood.
I ain't never let myself down, so far down, it feels impossible to pick
    myself up.
I ain't never been worried about today or tomorrow or about what
    happened yesterday.
I ain't never miss my uncle or wish we as a family tried harder to save him.
I ain't never felt pressure in the midst of such promise.
I ain't never felt ugly or at least strange-looking or at least not no
    one's type.
I ain't never really had a single bad day in my whole life.

I've only ever been hungry.

———————

Miles was hoping his mother was right this time. That this wasn't the
eraser shavings somehow trying to erase his sight, but that all this
was because

he was just hungry.

TIME, OUT

For lunch, the four of us
set our packets down
and make the trek to the cafeteria.

Brewton makes us walk single file, but Brad
don't care. He struts alongside
with his hand around Brewton's shoulder,

smirking at every other student walking by.
Alicia walks in front of me. She still smells like
everything I've ever wanted to smell, fresh even in

the stale of the day. Sandalwood heaven.
And behind me, gently knocking the side of his head
against the wall, a murmuring Tobin.

"I'm starving," Tobin said under his breath but loud enough for Miles to hear. "So hungry I could . . . eat a book."

"Why would you want to eat a book?" Miles groused. He wasn't actually talking to Tobin but was instead talking to himself about the strange thing he'd heard Tobin say.

It wasn't until they got to the entryway of the cafeteria that Miles rushed to hold the door for Alicia. He'd had the ripped-out page from the spider book in his hand, the note he'd written asking Alicia out, and was ready for the handoff. Ready to slide it in her hand as she walked by. Okay, it didn't go nearly as smooth as expected. It was awkward and almost a fumble because Alicia couldn't figure out why Miles was reaching for her hand. But she caught on and took the note, which had been folded small enough to disappear in her closed palm.

Miles held the door for Tobin, too. He wasn't planning on it, but Tobin took full advantage of the romance and chivalry meant for Alicia. And as he entered the cafeteria, passing Miles, Tobin responded to the question Miles had never actually asked him.

"Some books are better off in here"—Tobin pointed to his stomach—"than in here." He pointed to his head.

UH-HUH

Sometimes

when you call

a strange thing different,

you make room

for a different thing

to become dangerous.

———————

Sometimes, strange is just . . . strange.

Also.

Sometimes you're just too hungry to hear.

MENU

Everybody think
these fancy schools
got better lunches
than regular schools,
but the truth is, the

only thing different
be the salad bar.

Everything else is
chicken fingers,
cheeseburgers,
wings, pizza,
and curly fries.

As Miles stood at the condiment bar, drowning his food in ketchup and trying to figure out how to not be weird around Alicia, a kid named Reggie White came over to talk. Reggie was with Winnie Stockton.

"Alicia, remember what I told you this morning?" Winnie asked out the side of her mouth, because no one was supposed to be allowed to speak to the students in ISS. Alicia nodded. "Well, this is Reggie. They wanted to ask about the open mic and all that . . ."

Miles stepped away. Let them talk. Mainly because, if Reggie wanted to get involved with reciting poetry, Miles knew how embarrassing that could be. He'd almost worked up enough nerve to do it himself, just to impress Alicia. On the other hand, if Reggie was trying to get involved with *Alicia*, well, Miles didn't want to be anywhere near that.

Miles stood along the wall, waiting for Brewton to wrangle everyone. Brad talked as if he wasn't in suspension. Alicia was sneak-talking to Winnie and Reggie. And Tobin was talking to Mr. Chamberlain. Or, rather Mr. Chamberlain was talking to him. Straightening his tie. Patting his head.

FLAVOR

Cafeteria food don't taste
the same when it's not
in the cafeteria.

Maybe part of the seasoning
is that sour mop water and
salt in the air.

———————

Back in Room 501, Miles sat at his desk and gnawed on his chicken fingers, which, on that day, strangely tasted more like fingers than chicken. And his fries were gummy. The consistency of the teeth in his nightmare. And his soda flat.

Miles choked it all down anyway. Barely.

Alicia took a bite and pushed the rest of her wings to the side. Unfolded Miles's note, read it, and began scribbling a response.

Brad had a feast of all the fried offerings. But he ate little, if any at all—spent most of lunch slurping through his straw just for the annoying gurgling sound. The sound all their stomachs were making inside.

When Miles finally checked to see how Tobin's lunch was going, Tobin had peeled all the cheese off his pizza—a single glob—and ate it by itself as if it were skin.

TOBIN'S DRINK

I never seen no one
peel paper from a straw
by ripping the feet off,
then inching it from the
top with lip and teeth,
slurping and chewing
it like uncut pasta.

———————————

Miles waited for Tobin to spit the paper out. Instead, Tobin took a sip of his drink, swallowed it down. For a moment, a split second, Miles thought he saw something crawl from Tobin's nose, but Tobin sniffed it back up.

What the . . .

Gross.

Miles knew better. He knew it wasn't polite to stare, and he was so caught off guard by Tobin that he didn't even know he'd been locked on him. Until Tobin caught him.

Miles turned away.

"Your eyes okay, Miles?" Tobin asked. "You know vision is at the center of all we do."

Miles wasn't sure if that was meant to be joke or not. So he just didn't respond. Didn't look back. But his eyes began to burn.

180

SPIDER FACT

Spiders can sense
a particular electricity

in the air, shoot
silk web into it,

and ride the current
for miles and miles.

———————

At just the right time—which happened to be the exact moment
Miles began to rub his eyes again—a piece of . . . paper folded into
the size of a thumbnail came tumbling under Miles's desk. He looked
around, making sure Coach Holt and Brewton weren't paying attention, then, while pretending to tie his shoe, picked it up. He slowly
unfolded it in his lap. Read it. Could see it as clear as day.

YOU REALLY WILLING TO COME TO HARLEM? —A.C.

181

HARLEM FOR HER

The thing is,
everybody know
Brooklyn do
    and
Harlem do
     but
Brooklyn and Harlem don't
    together.

    However,

Alicia is the Apollo and the A and what's left
of the jazz spots. She a sax solo from so long ago
hummed on a stoop, and she also the hustlers and holler-ers
on the corner. She Two-Fifth, St. Nick, the park,
Central, and Morningside. She the African hair-braiders
and the heavy chains around somebody big brother neck,
who gets to play God until he meets God or makes good.
Alicia is the Renaissance and the book festival and the
Schomburg library. She the window the old ladies hang out of
to talk mess. She that. Casual conversation in code.
Alicia a whole world, and yet a whole world away from me,

    because

Brooklyn and Harlem don't
    together.
Everybody know that.
    But
I think it's time
Brooklyn and Harlem do.
Brooklyn and Harlem due.

BELL!

ENGLISH

PACKET

Bananas to the bottom.
Next up, a bug.

Miles tried focusing on the task in front of him. Not the . . . task beside him, tap-tap-tapping.

GREGOR SAMSA

There's this story my father
used to read to me.
Never at bedtime because it's
sort of the stuff of nightmares.

He would read it to me
in the morning, starting the
year I turned eleven. A wake-up
tale about the body changing

overnight, as the main character,
Gregor Samsa, a good man doing
the best he could, woke to find
he'd gone from man to insect.

———————————

This was how Miles's father talked to him about puberty. How he explained why Miles smelled like a foot or why there was hair growing where there hadn't been any before—except on his face—new tangles sprouting from the corners of his body. Why things were suddenly hard. And different.

PROMPT

*Read this story and,
in one page, write
about a time you woke
up a brand-new thing.*

———————

Uh-oh.

PERFECT

When I see Franz Kafka's
    The Metamorphosis,

I get excited because I know
this story forward and backward.
I also know all about Gregor feeling
trapped in a new self, him hiding
under the couch, and Mr. Kafka,
    whoever he was,

never explaining why this
might happen to someone,
and how I can never explain,
not even in an essay for
Ms. Blaufuss, why this has
    happened to me.

Miles tried to find a new angle. Maybe he could write about what it was like his freshman year at BVA and how he definitely felt changed. Or at least, he felt like everyone else saw him as something other than how he'd always seen himself. And not just the kids at his new school but also the kids in his neighborhood.

"Yo, you gotta wear church clothes to school?" Martell asked the first weekend Miles came back to the block. They'd always gone to the same school until Miles got into Brooklyn Visions Academy. Miles was happy to reply to Martell no, that he didn't have to wear "church clothes," which was Martell's way of saying, a uniform. If Miles had said yes, Martell would've teased him for not being able to get fly, and also probably would've questioned what it was like to wear a suit to school, even though it wasn't a suit. As if Miles might feel more important wearing those kinds of clothes.

Miles considered what it was like the first time Alicia spoke to him. How he felt changed then. Or even how he felt changed now, just because she'd written him back. Like someone could see him, at least, that's what he'd hoped. The truth was, Miles was playing the long game. The longest game ever. Because he had no game. At all. But Alicia knew that. She knew. And Miles knowing she knew and knowing she didn't say no was enough to make him feel new.

Or maybe he could've written about Ms. Blaufuss and how she'd introduced him to poetry. Miles never thought he'd like something like . . . poetry. But he did. Because it taught him how a little can do a lot.

Poems were like smaller bangs. Making many new worlds.

STARTLED

Weird how in a quiet room,
the childish chime of a

cell phone someone forgot
to set on silent sounds like

a siren.

UH-OH.

Miles thought he'd made sure his phone was on silent, but he must've forgotten to do it when he was going down the checklist of things to make sure of for In-School Suspension. You know, nothing unbuttoned. Nothing out of place. Nothing human. Check, check, check.

Not to mention, who would've been texting him, anyway? This was an interesting question but not nearly as interesting as Miles's response. Startled, he flinched, slamming his hand against the desk, immediately afraid he'd break another one. But he didn't. But you know how hands are, they're always connected to wrists. And this *particular* hand was connected to a *particular* wrist. The *buttoned* wrist. The one wearing . . . the web-shooter.

A wad of web no bigger than a single stick of chewed gum shot from under Miles's sleeve across the room, sticking to the front of Coach Holt's desk.

It all happened so fast, perhaps at the pace of Miles's heartbeat, as he braced himself for what he just couldn't explain. Everyone's eyes darted forward thinking they saw something in their periphery but not sure they saw anything. And before anyone could study too long . . .

A KNOCK AT THE DOOR

A face peering through
the cell window, like a
puppy left in a car.

Scratching for attention,
everyone looks as Brewton
opens up and in comes

Ganke.

Miles watched as Ganke bopped over to Coach Holt's desk, a folder
in hand, and even though Miles could only see the side of Ganke's
face, he could tell he was sporting a goofy smirk. Ganke style.

A FOOL

You okay? Ganke mouthed.
I nodded.

I was talking to Alicia, Ganke mouthed.
I scowled.

But you okay? Ganke mouthed again.
I nodded.

I was talking to— he mouthed, but was cut off.
Shown the door.

"Ganke!" Brewton snapped, the sound of his voice sending a shock through Ganke's body.

"I'm leaving, I'm leaving," Ganke said. He tried mouthing to Miles again.

"Now!" Brewton barked.

GANKE CODE

I was talking to
means

he was talking to
me.

———————

Miles needed to figure out how to check his phone. That text message had to have been from Ganke.

And had to have been important.

NEW ASSIGNMENT

Coach Holt passes out new worksheets.
They're from Ms. Blaufuss,
who apparently has a change
of plans. We're now supposed to
read a shorter short story called
"Girl." Just "Girl." By someone named
Jamaica Kincaid. A good name.

Before attempting the new assignment for Ms. Blaufuss, Miles tried to first figure out how to ease his cell phone from his pocket so he could see the text message.

Coach Holt wasn't a problem. Her head was still buried in the newspaper. She was only about halfway through it, and it was clear she was planning on reading the whole thing. But Brewton, well, he was a problem. Not as much of a problem as he could've been only because he was caught in some sort of euphoric trance, the music in his ears blaring loud enough to sound like a bug zapper to everyone else in the room.

Alicia raised her hand, but Coach Holt's head was down. And instead of calling for her to get her attention, Alicia decided to go right to the source of distraction.

"Brewton, you mind?" Alicia asked.

"Whatchusay?" Brewton stopped swaying, removed one of his earbuds. Miles aborted his cell phone mission immediately.

"We can hear your music," Alicia explained. "It's distracting."

"What you listening to, anyway?" Brad followed.

"Mind your business," Brewton replied.

"Come on, man, it's loud enough for you to be making it our business," Brad said.

"Seriously," Alicia murmured.

"Some of us are trying to work. I mean . . . not me and clearly not you either, but . . . Alicia is!"

"Stop playing with me, Canby," Brewton grunted, screwing the earbud back into his head.

JAMAICA

I never been to Jamaica,
but I've been to Flatbush.
I've had my fair share of
meat patties. And also I've
waited in line for chicken
from a drum. And I've
always loved that the fried
fish comes with dumplings
called festival, which seems
to me to be a more fitting
name for a dumpling than
dumpling, which makes me
wonder if Jamaica is a more
fitting name for the writer
of this story than any other
name. Even though I haven't
been there, I wonder if it's like
a sunnier Flatbush Avenue,
complete with musical voices
and bodies that play and mouths
that don't. So if that's anything
like Jamaica, is this person
a Jamaica like I am a Miles?

Is she an island like I am a journey?

Miles glanced at the story, which was only a page long, and before he could begin reading it, Brad piped up again.

"I can't even concentrate on reading because your music blasting, Brewton!"

"It ain't blasting!"

"Just tell me what it is," Brad whined. "And then I'm gonna do my work. I swear."

"It's Funkadelic," Brewton said.

"Why you talking about Miles like that," Brad joked.

"*Shhhh,*" Alicia shushed.

"That's the name of the song?" Brad asked.

"*Shhhh,*" Alicia shushed again.

"No, that's the name of the group," Brewton said.

"*Shhhhhh!*" From Alicia, now louder.

"Quiet down, everyone," Coach Holt said finally. "Back to work."

"Okay, okay, Coach," Brad said. "But seriously, can you first get Brewton to tell me what song he jammin' to over there? I gotta know."

Coach Holt shook her head over Brad's shenanigans and huffed. "Brewton, just tell him, please."

Brewton huffed, shook his head. "It's called 'America Eats Its Young.'"

Brad thought for a moment, searching for a joke. But couldn't find one.

INSTRUCTIONS

*Read this story and, using the erasure technique, answer one of these
    questions:*

What did you find interesting about the way it's written?
Do you relate at all to the speaker or who's being spoken to? If so, why?

*NOTE: A semicolon is meant to separate closely related ideas in the
    same sentence.*

―――――――――

Miles sighed, read on.

"GIRL"

I have to read it
a few times and maybe
a few times after that,
and still don't know if

I read it   right.

From what I can tell,
a girl is being told by
her mother what she
has to do in order to be.

———————

At first Miles thought the dust in his eyes—which, for whatever reason, wouldn't seem to leave him alone—was messing up the way punctuation looked on the page. Like the periods were blurring into semicolons. But after reading it again and again, he realized it was just written that way.

PERIOD

The whole story only one sentence.

Just one long sentence with 51 semicolons,

a few commas, a few question marks,

but not a period nowhere.

Not one. And Miles was relieved but confused.

;

I don't really get the semicolon,
only because it don't seem to do nothing
a comma or a period don't do,

which makes me wonder why this
Jamaica lady ain't just use 51 periods,
and why she thought this had to be

one sentence. Even though when
my father is telling me all the things
about how I need to be, he don't

insert many periods either. Just goes
on and on and on and on and on,
barely breathing between ons.

And when my mother does it,
it don't sound quite as mean, but she
don't even hit the space bar in her brain.

―――――――

Miles tried not to be distracted by Tobin's tapping, though it had
been bothering him the majority of the day. Was Tobin anxious or
just annoying? Either way, the tap-tap-tapping continued, and in this
moment, Miles didn't mind it as much, only because it made sense
to keep rhythm with this particular story.

AGAIN

I read it again; word after word; trying to make sense of it; trying to find something I felt like I might've been missing; *always eat your food in such a way it won't turn someone else's stomach*; which means what?; *this is how to make a buttonhole for the button you have just sewed on*; how she know?; *this is how you smile to someone you don't like too much*; why should I smile?; *don't throw stones at blackbirds, because it might not be a blackbird at all*; I get this, I think; *this is how a man bullies you*; this; this;

this?

———————

There were lines about spitting up in the air, and throwing away children, and squeezing bread.

But there was one Miles kept getting caught up on.

this is how you sweep a corner;

CORNERS

I understand why a person might sweep corners
and wipe clear what don't bother as part
of thoroughly cleaning a house.

But I have to wonder why so much gathers at
the meeting points of a building, where the walls
kiss and become strong.

I have to wonder why that nook magnetizes
the gentle throwaways, gives them space for
their own universes.

———————

This, Miles thought after the fourth reading.

BZZZ!

I try reading it a fifth time,
"Girl" by Jamaica Kincaid,
but there is suddenly an
ocean in my stomach, and
a beach in my throat, and
a pepper or two in my blood.

———————

Miles, on high alert, noticed that on the edge of the desk was another one. Another termite. He leaned in to make sure he was seeing what he was seeing, and once he realized he was, he smashed the bug under his thumb.

When he sat back, the chair came apart beneath him, the legs of it crumbling. And as Miles crashed to the floor, thousands of termites came from the chair—from inside of it—scattering everywhere.

SCREAM

I don't know much about termites.
Not like I know about spiders.

I also don't know much about screaming
at a thousand little things that seem to be

trying to eat me, live in me, hollow me out.
Not because I don't know much about a thousand

little things that seem to be trying to eat me,
but because I don't know much about screaming.

———————

Miles yelped as he hit the floor. Everyone assumed it was because of the fall, but it was because of the termites. But it didn't take long for Miles to realize no one else could see them. That they weren't actually there.

"Miles, you okay?" Alicia said, quickly jumping from her seat to help him.

Coach Holt jumped up as well. Came to the other side of her desk to see what had happened.

Brad tittered once he realized Miles was okay.

Brewton left the room, went to grab a broom to get up the shards of wood.

Tobin didn't move. Just continued scribbling on his worksheet.

EVERYTHING IS BRUISED

You ever wanted to
pull your face off and
fold it up and tuck it

in your pocket so no
one knows it's glowing
in neon embarrassment,

bright enough to blind
the people you think

think you cool?

————————

Coach Holt got Miles a new chair. And though Miles came out physi-
cally unscathed, Coach Holt asked him if he was okay again, which
might as well have been the most painful splinter. The one that
lodged itself into his ego.

"Shake it off," Brewton grunted, sweeping up the last of the
chair bits. The bigger pieces of wood, he'd already picked up. Miles
nodded. Tried to forget it all. The fall. The colony of termites he
saw, then didn't see. He eased into the new chair, pulled back up
to the desk, back up to his English work, what Ms. Blaufuss had in
store, what Jamaica Kincaid had to say, back to the erasure poem,
and hoped he could erase this from his mind. More importantly, he
hoped Alicia could erase it from hers.

A COMPLICATED LESSON FROM MS. BLAUFUSS

Sometimes we erase things
to create new meaning in what once was.

Other times we erase things
to be demeaning to what once was.

The way you know the difference
is in the ease in which you do it.

———————————

Miles searched for himself in the words Jamaica Kincaid had provided.
He wasn't sure there would be anything for him, but Ms. Blaufuss
always said you have to believe in magic in order to recognize a spell.

RESPONSE TO MS. BLAUFUSS'S OTHER QUESTION

I can relate to the girl in "Girl"; an erasure poem:

hold up

someone else's

directions

and

crease

your throat

and

throw away

something you

love

air

Miles finished his erasure poem, and when he started to read over it, the words he'd left uncovered started disappearing: *hold up someone else's directions and crease your throat* . . .

Blink.   Blink.   *Bzzz!*

Three termites scurried across Miles's desk. He slammed his hand on them.

Wham!

A hairline crack eked through across the surface of the wood. *Oh, no, not again,* Miles thought, the broken desk that landed him in detention crossing his mind.

Then, as everyone jumped, startled by the bang, Miles raised his hand as if he didn't do it.

"Yes, Miles?" Coach Holt said, one hand on her heart.

"I, um . . . can I . . . I need to use the bathroom."

HALLWAY

There is no one in the hallway
except two students,
    Winnie and that kid,
what's their name, Reggie.
I know their name's Reggie.
But you know.

I don't know

what they're doing in the hallway,
hanging posters all up and down the wall.
    Maybe running
for homecoming court or
student government or
whatever

other vote-for-me there is. Or maybe
they're overachievers given
    the busy work
of beautifying bulletin boards
instead of being bored in class.

I don't know.
I don't care.

———————

Miles couldn't think of anything, except for what he already knew.
What he could already feel. But he had to wait until he was in the
bathroom to confirm it.

LOSING IT

Brewton walks me
like I'm a little boy,
but when we get
there, he treats me
like I'm contagious.

Waits outside, earbuds
in, frowning like this
the worst part of
his job but the best
part of the song.

I splash water on
my face, tell myself
to pull it together.
Then I hear tap-tap-
tapping until Tobin

is behind me. Slack
jaw, mouth a deep
cave. I turn around,
but he's gone. Look
around, but he's gone.

Even the bathrooms at Brooklyn Visions Academy were elegant. Sophisticated. Smart. Besides the strange piss troughs that lined the walls—which were mosaic tile—everything else was made of rich cherrywood, including the walls and doors of the bathroom stalls. And if it weren't for the teenage boys always inhabiting the space, it could've easily been mistaken for a cigar lounge.

Miles, flustered, leaned into a corner, hovering over what seemed to be a tiny pile of dirt, maybe sawdust—something like that—and pulled his cell phone from his pocket.

ONE NEW MESSAGE:

FROM GANKE 12:43 p.m.:
(MORE VERSIONS)

Bro, that kid Tobin in there with you? People talking about him. They say they found all these books under his bed, but that was after Tripley caught him taking them. That's what sparked the whole room raid. But the raid ain't the important part. Guess what I heard he was doing when Tripley caught him? Guess, Miles. Guess! Guess! HE WAS EATING THEM! MILES, TOBIN WAS EATING THE PAGES OUT OF THE BOOKS!

———————

Miles read the text over and over again before starting to text Ganke back.

FROM MILES 1:13 p.m.

WHAT?! I KNEW SOMETHING WAS—

"Hurry it up in there!" Brewton barked through the door. Miles, spooked, dropped his phone in the sink. Thankfully, there was no water in it to damage it, but that was enough to scare him into putting his phone away.

When he came from the bathroom, Miles's shirt was wet, and his face looked like he'd seen something he wasn't supposed to see, which is never a good face, especially when coming from a bathroom.

"You good, Big Man?" Brewton asked.

"Yeah," Miles grunted, looking behind him. And as they headed back down the hall, Miles looked over his shoulder again. And once more after that.

BACK IN CLASS

I glance at Tobin,
still at his desk,

    scribbling scribbling,

making an inkblot
of his worksheet,

    scribbling scribbling,

turning the Jamaica lady's story
into damn near nothing.

———————

Miles, now certain something's up with Tobin, gets lost in his imagination playing out what might be a showdown, but how in this one
room?

<THE WAY I IMAGINE IT>

<I stun the entire class
with a venom blast.
Send it through the floor
so no one knows
it's coming.

Then I'd vanish.

Blend right in to
the desks and chair
and walls of this room.

I don't know what Tobin is capable of.

I don't know if he has powers.
I don't even know
if he's actually sinister, but I know
something is off. Something
is dangerously different.

I honestly don't think
this would require anything more
than a bit of web
around his hands and feet,
at least to start, because

I don't know what Tobin is capable of.

But I know
no one knows—
it's coming.>

Miles, envisioning an altercation with Tobin, tried his best to not lead on. To not be obvious.

And after he'd snapped out of it, trying his best not to be chastised by Coach Holt again—he knew he was on thin ice—he glanced over to see what Tobin, the book eater, was up to.

t

e

r

might

220

As Tobin finished scratching out the words to the story, his brows knit together in concentration, his lips slightly parted, a termite danced in the corner of his mouth. With his tongue, he swiped it, keeping it from crawling out. He didn't chew. He didn't swallow. Just let it live in his mouth.

TERMITE FACT, I THINK (IN TRIPLEY'S VOICE)

The etymology of termite is interesting because it's made up of two words. The first is *ter*, which is short for *ter*rifying, or *ter*rible. And the second is *mite*. Which translates, in some language I can't remember and maybe never learned, to something like nasty, itchy bug. Or big disgusting monster. Or something like that.

At this point, for Miles, the question was no longer what? Or, who? It was only, how? And, when?

BELL!

HISTORY

ON DAYS LIKE TODAY (TUESDAY AFTERNOON)

I wish I was:

    Alicia Carson,
    Brad Canby,
    Tobin Rogers (when he was just Tobin),
    or even Miles Morales (when I was just Miles).

Anything (anyone)
other than

    Spider-Man.

Miles felt like his brain was splitting in half. One side concerned about who or what Tobin had become, and the other side concerned about what kind of work Mr. Chamberlain had assigned.

He thought, again, about what led him there. What strange circumstance landed him in suspension. And even though he was proud of what he'd done, proud he'd stood up for himself, proud he wouldn't allow himself to work from the floor, it was still unfair. Unfair enough to *not* have to do whatever work Mr. Chamberlain had assigned.

But he was in no position to stage another protest.

A REMINDER

I'm only here
for telling the truth.

I'm only here
because when you

upset or upstage or
upside-down

any authority figures,
like teachers who

can't figure out who
you are but think

they know who you are,
and don't know you

know who you are,
they name you a

bigmouth boy,
a trouble, a lie.

———————

Miles bit down hard on his bottom lip, tried not to worry about
Tobin, and turned the page to see what Chamberlain had in store.

LITERACY AND THE ENSLAVED

A TROUBLE;

Between 1740 and 1834, many slaveholding states throughout the South passed laws preventing enslaved people from learning to read and write. The fear was that enslaved Africans who could read and write might be able to forge their own freedom documents. Might be able to read and write themselves free.

———————

Miles read the paragraph on the worksheet, but, as had been happening since the eraser dust incident, which Miles now knew wasn't an accident, his eyes began to itch, and at times felt like they were crossing.

But this time, the words didn't fade. This time, right in front of his face, right there on the worksheet, the letters began to change and rearrange. Into:

A LIE;

In 1619, and some would argue even before then,
Africans had no desire to read and write simply
because they, as savages, didn't have brains big
enough for such complex tasks. To try and teach
them would be cruel, because it would convince them
of the impossible: that they deserved to be free.

———————————

Miles blinked.

Blink,   blinked.   Blinked the worksheet back to its original words. . . . *Might be able to read themselves free.*

Gathered himself. Then read Mr. Chamberlain's instructions for the assignment.

Deep breath.

A TROUBLE;

How do you think Brooklyn Visions Academy
should teach you to read and write yourself free?

———————

Again, the letters began to shape-shift and reorganize on the page. Into:

A LIE;

How do you think Brooklyn Visions Academy
should work to civilize you?

———————————

What? Miles thought, squinting his eyes, trying to make sure he was seeing what he was seeing.
Civilize me?

Miles turned to see if Alicia was seeing the same thing on her paper.

But she didn't seem bothered. Hadn't looked up.

Miles blinked. Blinked twice. Blinked a third time   and the words had changed again. Into:

A LIE;

*Why do you think Brooklyn Visions Academy
should ban you from its classrooms?*

This time the letters, in their changing, didn't dance into new sentences. Instead, they began to crawl, each of the alphabet scampering off the page toward Miles.

Miles jumped again, this time springing from his seat, almost ramming his knee straight up and through his desk.

"Big Man," Brewton snarled. "Sit."

Miles tried to compose himself.

"Everything okay, Miles?" Coach Holt asked. Miles just nodded and eased back down onto his chair.

"Miles," Alicia whispered. He turned his head just enough to catch her eye. "You good?"

A TROUBLE.

———————————

"Shhhhhhhh!" Tobin hissed.

Miles blinked again, this time longer, this time squeezing his eyes shut for a ten-count before opening them.

Mr. Chamberlain's instructions had reconstructed:

How do you think Brooklyn Visions Academy
should teach you to read and write yourself free?

Miles flipped the worksheet over so he wouldn't be distracted by any other changes that might've occurred. Overcome with anger, though certain Mr. Chamberlain would probably not even read it (busy work), he decided to give this answer everything he had.

Rio Morales style.

TO ANSWER MR. CHAMBERLAIN'S QUESTION:

A RECKONING

It is impossible
for words to change
before my eyes
and for meaning
to shift under me
like land separating
violently, yet so
quietly, I would
miss it if I weren't
watching, like how
no one ever hears
a fly once it's caught
in a web, once its
buzzing is out of
earshot, and it waits
for its life to be chewed.
Being eaten is nothing
I dream of. To be stuck
is not a thing I've desired.

———————————

Miles paused, glanced at the scar left from the spider bite. Then over at Tobin.

He went on.

———————————

But I do understand
how webs work.

I do know how an abstract
ghost-like substance

can come from inside you
and be made into a physical

thing. How you could birth
a trap you ain't even know

you had in you, built from
a life punctured by weird

punctuation, semicolons, and
jagged fragments, a life

patterned after the most ridiculous
tales and the truths of nature.

His hand slightly trembling, he went on.

If tributaries all depend on
        how the land moves downhill;
and lightning is formed from an
        imbalance between cloud and
ground; and tree limbs grow
        wild, chasing the sun's energy,

and their fruit adapt to the living
        and dying things around them,
why should we be any different
        than products of our environment,
our imbalances, and our need
        to be close to what energizes us?

———————

Miles could feel the blood coursing through his veins and was gripping the pen with such force that when he looked down at his forearm, his veins were so engorged they could be seen through the cotton of his sleeve.

Same. Pattern.

He went on.

———————

But also, who am I to believe
I can't create my own patterns.

That I can't build my own map,
leading me to my own dream.

Or lay track for my own train,
high voltage beneath the surface.

Nothing's strong enough to stop it
from reaching where it's headed.

It's not a runaway, but mistaken for one
because it rattles and sparks

and screams. Better yet, who am I
to believe, whether you believe it or not,

that I can't write my own story,
and read it to the world?

———————————

Now his hand was shaking. But still he went on.

And who are you,
Mr. Chamberlain,

but an ugly equation,
a mess of numbers and letters
we can't seem to solve?

A repetitive pattern in nature
that in any other context would
be a cliché?

A paper doll? A wooden trinket
on the mantel of madness?

The question isn't whether or
not this place teaches us to
dig ourselves from the graves
of ignorance and fear,
read and write ourselves free.

The question is why do you,
Mr. Chamberlain, so desperately
want to bury us alive?

———————

Miles, though his hand was practically vibrating, was satisfied with
this answer. He flipped the worksheet back over only to find the
words still running around like agitated insects.

GOLDEN RULE

My mother wears
gold necklaces.
Tiny links carrying
the weight of Jesus
and her name.

She's always loved yellow
gold, and once I bought
her a bracelet from a
hustler on Fulton who
told me he'd usually
move it for thirty, but
because it was me, even
though he ain't know me,
he'd let it go for ten and
some change.

It had charm, I thought,
plus charms dangling from
it like kindergarten
construction-paper
mobiles: a heart, a
lightning bolt,
my initials, and some
other pieces reminiscent
of Monopoly.

It turned green in three days.
Left a ring around her wrist,
a second bracelet the color
of my embarrassment.
That day I learned if it turns
or tarnishes, it ain't real.

Miles thought about this as the words on his paper changed. He knew this couldn't have been real. But how could he be sure?

Miles raised his hand.

"Yes, Miles," Coach Holt said.

"Sorry, but there's something wrong with my paper," Miles said, holding it up. Coach Holt didn't bother getting up, but she did lean in and squint.

"Looks fine to me, Miles," she said. "Everybody's worksheet good, right?"

"Mine's fine, I guess," Brad said, uninterested.

"Same," Alicia said matter-of-factly.

EXTRA

Tobin holds his paper up
so Coach Holt can see the black
printed on the white, curves and
crosses and dots and loops.

Apparently identical language
as the others, words that
somehow have been skittering
around, leaving me to think

I'm losing it on the longest
day of my life. Tobin hands
me his paper; a smirk smears
too wide to be sincere.

"See?"

It was then Miles realized Tobin had no business even having a work-sheet.

He wasn't even in this class.

He wasn't even in this class. He wasn't even in this class.

He wasn't even in this class. He wasn't even in this class. He wasn't even in this class.

He wasn't even in this class. He wasn't even in this class. He wasn't even in this class. He wasn't even in this class.

But Miles looked at it anyway.

Savage. Savage. Savage. Savage. Savage. Savage. Savage. Savage.
Savage. Savage. Savage. Savage. Savage. Savage. Savage. Savage.
Savage. Savage. Savage. Savage. Savage. Savage. Savage. Savage.
Savage. Savage. Savage. Savage. Savage. Savage. Savage. Savage.

Savage. Savage. Savage. Savage. Savage. Savage. Savage. Savage.
Savage. Savage. Savage. Savage. Savage. Savage. Savage. Savage.
Savage. Savage. Savage. Savage. Savage. Savage. Savage. Savage.
Savage. Savage. Savage. Savage. Savage. Savage. Savage. Savage.

Breath shot from Miles's body, not like a yawn, like a yell. Or a yelp. But without sound.

I BLINK

Savage. Savage. Savage. Savage. Savage. Savage. Savage. Savage. Savage. Savage. Savage. Savage. Savage.

Savage. Savage. Savage. Savage. Savage. Savage. Savage. Savage. Savage. Savage. Savage. Savage. Savage.

Savage. Savage. Savage. Savage. Savage. Savage. Savage. Savage. Savage. Savage. Savage. Savage. Savage.

Blink.

s p i d e r.

And now that's all the paper said. 234 letters, blurred into six.

Spider.

I BLINK AGAIN

and Tobin's face is
a bed of termites,
his birthmark now
a splash of critters.

———————

Miles flung the worksheet back at Tobin. Then, without even bothering to raise his hand, blurted,

"I gotta go the bathroom." He was already half out of his seat.

"You just went, Miles," Coach Holt replied skeptically.

"I know, but . . ." Miles held his stomach. "I . . . gotta go."

"It's probably the chicken fingers," Brad offered with a shrug.

BATHROOM; BREAK

I feel like
an engine
with no car,
a motor on
the sidewalk,
revvvvving.

————————

Though Miles was in a panic, he still understood that he'd need to make sure Brewton wouldn't come looking for him, so as they approached the bathroom, Miles shot a few quick web-loogies on the floor. That way, once Brewton stepped in them, he'd be stuck. Also, once Miles pushed the door of the bathroom open, he webbed it shut behind him.

BACK TO THE SINK

Water. Splash.
Water. Splash.

Eyes. Open.
No one. Here.

No one there.

STALL

I sit on the commode,
everything up and on,
to try to catch my breath.

Try to make sense of my
sense that something is
happening. And then:

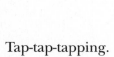

_____

Tap-tap-tapping.

Tap-tap-tapping coming from behind him. Miles slipped into camouflage, blending in with the white bowl and rich reddish brown of the
back wall. He unbuttoned his unwebbed sleeve to expose his shooter.
Listened. Listened.

> Listened. To what they'd always called the monsters
> behind the wall.
> And waited.

TAP TAP

Tap   Tap

   Tap   Tap

Tap Tap Tap Tap Tap

Tap Tap

Tap Tap

Tap

Tap Tap Tap Tap

Tap Tap Tap

Tap Tap Tap

Tap Tap Tap

Tap Tap Tap

The tapping was coming from behind the toilet. A chip of wood, no bigger than a hole punch, pushed out first.

WALL

I'm not sure what
    I am looking at.
Is the wall

      buckling up?
  Caving in?
      Coming down?

———————

Then, Miles saw something small moving around on the other side of the hole. An insect like a grain of rice eating at the wood. A termite. Every few seconds it would knock its head against the wood, causing a tapping sound.

WHICH, AGAIN, MAKES ME THINK

It's never said
just how many
feet we are from all
the other feet of
all the other skittering
and scattering things.

Not to mention their eyes.
Not to mention their teeth.

———————

Right before Miles's eyes, as dust crumbs fell onto the porcelain
commode, the jagged opening expanded little by little. Whatever
was behind it was hungry.

AND SO IT BEGINS (THE WAY IT ACTUALLY HAPPENS)

First, there is only one.

But as that one comes crawling through
the hole it has eaten in the wood,

the rest of the wall begins to pimple
and dot like a teenage face.

Of a teenage face.

———————————

Miles was horrified. Backed himself against the stall door. Hands up.
Fists tight. Up on the balls of his feet. Ready. For whatever.

NERVOUS SYSTEM (*BZZZ!*)

You ever hear your heartbeat
play a solo, and you know it ain't
showing off, it's just forgotten the song?

You ever feel your breath thicken
in your body, make you feel like
you breathing gravy?

You ever feel your jaw
lock around your tongue
and become a closed   trunk,

only because I don't want to say casket
right now. Not right now. Not when I feel
like blood is coursing
through my body and my body
is corpsing at the same time.

The next bite was the biggest. A chomp that took out the whole middle of the wall. And there was Tobin—Tobin?—his face no different than it had been. Big head. Awkwardly kind-looking. Birthmark. Goofy glasses. Until. Pincers grew from his mouth.

"How . . . are you here, *and* . . . in class?" Miles asked, which immediately seemed like a ridiculous question.

BIRTHMARK

Whenever I looked in Tobin's face:

I usually saw a one-winged moth.

Or from New York to Georgia
and as far west as the Mississippi.

A piece of apple pie, not a slice,
a piece snatched from the pan.

A puddle in a pothole.

A ripped cover of a strange book.

Now his birthmark had become an
island occupied by ravenous vermin.

His face a feast for them.

———————————

"Who . . . *what* are you?" Miles asked, his web-shooter at the ready. Brewton, completely unaware that his feet were probably stuck to the floor, was singing at the top of his lungs on the other side of the bathroom door. "America Eats Its Young," on repeat.

VERSIONS

The thing about Tobin,
about this version of him,

(because school is all about versions)

is that even though he looks
just like himself, the him still sitting in class,

his face is now three times the size,
the birthmark of mites, alive,
his mouth, which is already a junk

drawer of strange utensils, is now
a scrapyard of sharp teeth.

———————

"I . . . am the secret that lives all around you," Tobin snarls in a voice
not his own. His voice was soft. Very much made for the library. But
this voice was a voice that sounded like it had been . . . eating wood.
"The original bookworm."

"But . . . they let you out of class?"

"No, no, I'm there. Sorta," Tobin said. "Think of that version of
me as a . . . bookmark." Just then, Tobin began crawling from the
wall, pushing one arm through before another.

Then another.

Then another.

Four arms and two legs all squeezing through the jagged hole as if his
bones had gone gelatinous.

WEIRD (WHAT TOBIN IS CAPABLE OF)

He hisses to me
that he used to live
along the floorboards
of the Warden's house.
Also in the foundation
of the prisons. And
even in the molding
of the school.

But now he stays in the
woodgrain of Mr. Chamberlain's
desk. Or nestled in his textbooks
of sideways history,
and even in the pencils
tucked behind his ear.

The ones he uses to
fail me or wrongfully write me,
with this wicked wood,
into wrongdoing.

———————

Tobin lifted two of his arms, swung them at Miles's face as if trying to
clap his head between his hands, his pincers jutting from his mouth.
Miles ducked, just barely evading a crushing round of applause.

"What . . . why . . . what do you want from me?" Miles asked.

WHAT PEOPLE WANT FROM ME

My father: everything (he wants)
My mother: everything (she wants)
My block: anything (I have)

Austin: a thought
Ganke: a laugh
Alicia: hopefully, something

Dean Kushner: a mascot
Ms. Blaufuss: a feeling
Mr. Chamberlain: a failure

Tobin:

"What do I want from you?" Tobin mocked. "What do I want from you? Can't you see you're in the way?"

"In the way of what? What are you talking about?" Miles was still on guard, waiting for the inevitable to happen. On the other side of the door, he could hear Brewton speaking to someone in the hallway. Probably another student dawdling, trying to avoid class. Or maybe he was talking to himself, cussing out whatever kid stickied the floor.

"Let me ask you something," Tobin said. "What makes you think books are going to do anything for your hoodlum cousin, Austin? He's a lost cause. Just like your uncle and most of your neighborhood and . . . you."

"How you even know about Austin?"

"We're everywhere." Tobin cackled, his birthmark grossly crawling around his face. "*Everywhere.* And we always know where our food is."

He snapped at Miles again.

FOOD

This time he barely misses my ear,
tries to bend me at my corner,
        dog-ear me

so I can keep my place.

———————

Miles checked him, put his forearm right where Tobin's Adam's apple would have been if he had been human, to back him up. Miles hoped he wasn't the "food" Tobin was talking about. But . . . kinda figured he was.

"But first, snowflake, I need you to die."

ANOTHER THING ABOUT SNOWFLAKES

They are not just soft.

When they begin to melt, they

harden into sleet.

———————————

Tobin shrilled, lunging toward Miles and grabbing him by his neck-
tie with two hands. And before Miles could swing, Tobin took hold
of Miles's wrists with his *other* two hands. Miles struggled as Tobin
snatched him, trying to wrestle his wrists loose while bobbing away
from the pincers. There were ribbons of shredded book pages
attached to each clapperclaw. And they were big enough to snip
Miles's head off.

IN THE WALL

Tobin yanks and yanks,
drags me through the hole
he'd made in the wall,
flinging me into the
innards of the school,

like being pulled
through the navel of
a building only to find
bugs in its belly, whittling
some kind of warped world

in the splintered wood.
It's all stabbing me, a gauntlet of
sawdusty stakes, pipes and wires,
beams and sharp clouds
ready to rain fiberglass.

And whatever else is meant
to insulate this vaulted place.
Whatever else is meant
to keep energy down
and voices muffled.

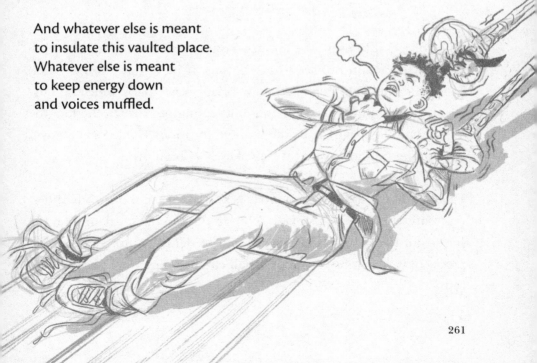

Miles brushed himself off, the not–cotton candy irritating his skin. He glanced around to see where he was. If he didn't know he was inside the wall, he'd think he was in a giant crawl space, wide enough to juke, tall enough to jump, and long enough to stretch the length of the building. Similar to the strange locations Ganke was always schlepping him to to find rare sneakers in Chinatown.

Tobin rushed Miles, all arms and legs and snapping things, but Miles was ready this time. He kicked Tobin in the thorax, hard enough to send him staggering back onto a pile of debris, pulverized books, pieces of wall that had been only half eaten. Gnawed-on plaster and frame.

I WASTED NO TIME, SHOT MY SHOT

-.-. . -. ... --- .-. ... .-. / .. ... / - .... .
/ -.-. ....-.. -.. / --- ..-. / ..-. . .- .-. / .-
-. -.. / - .... . / ..-. .- - .... . .-. / --- ..-. / ..
--. -. --- .-. .- -. -.-. .

Miles shot his web, let it spiral from his wrist, a projectile of silk. But it got caught up on the wooden stakes, the fractured foundational beams coming from the floor like giant nails. Imagine unraveling yarn in a briar patch. A snagged mess.

Relentless and now agitated, Tobin charged toward Miles again. But because Miles only had a single web-shooter—the other was tucked under his bed in his dorm room—he had to think quickly. So he cut the just-slung line and shot for the sky.

                                    up!
                          up
                                    up
                              up
                                    up
                              up
                                    up
                              up
                                    up
                              up
                        up
                                    up
                        up
                                    up
                    up
                        up
                    up
                        up
                    up
                        up
                    up
                        up
            up
                up
            up
                up
        Up

264

The web adhered to a support beam stretching across the rafter, each of the mooring threads like fingers gripping the wood high above them. Miles would've normally used his other shooter to either swing to a more advantageous position for a better attack or to go on the chase and plan a setup. But neither of those were options, so instead, he just figured the best thing to do was to climb, as fast as he could, as high as he could.

After climbing what must have been a few floors behind the wall, Miles stopped abruptly to survey around him. He'd climbed high enough to have the upper hand, but . . . not for long.

Tobin, with all his arms and legs and teeth, came darting up the wall after him.

SUSPENDED

I climbed fist over fist
up the web, like third-grade
gym-class rope races to the
ceiling, back when my biceps
were spitballs and my legs
would lock around the rope
at the ankles and my gym teacher,
whose name in this moment
escapes me, was yelling two things:

1. Use your feet, Miles. Use your feet!
2. No looking down! No looking down!

———————————

Of course, Miles looked down.

Tobin was coming.

WHEN HE'S CLOSE

Just beneath me,
he starts snipping at me,
his mandible clawing into
the rubber of my soles.

I turn my feet into fists.
Kick and kick and kick
my heel into the head
of this hideous thing.

Tobin fell to the floor.

Silence. Besides Miles's breathing.

Miles hung there, relieved just for a moment, while mapping his next move.

It was dark behind the wall. Dank. And the light pouring through the holes Tobin made in the stall lit the space. Casted shadows. Miles's was long and lean, but Tobin's, with all his arms, looked more like a spaceship descending upon Miles. Until it vanished in the rubble below. But the thing about termites is they're never alone. Ever. *If you see one, there are a thousand more.* So that one big spaceship was soon joined by a few smaller ones, their shadows inching up the wall, attacking Miles before their bodies did. And then a few more. And a few more, the room polka-dotting right before Miles's eyes.

TERMITE FACT (ACCORDING TO MR. TRIPLEY, AND THE COMMERCIALS)

For every person,
there's like a thousand pounds
of termites.

Pounds.

I don't know how many
people are in the world,
but based on what Mr. Tripley
be saying, I bet there are
enough termites to

weigh what the whole
world weighs.

Tobin climbed from the shadows again, this time skittering up the dark side of the room. Miles tried to use the same tactic and kick Tobin off of him, but this time he couldn't.

"Not this time, snowflake!" Tobin jeered. "Once you're out of the way, me and all the Chamberlains can finally finish the Warden's job and restore order."

With two hands holding Miles's feet, Tobin used his pincers to snap at Miles's face.

Snap! Miles shifted left, the pincers barely missing him.

"No more protests."

Snap! Miles shifted right, evading the claw once more.

"No more lying books."

Snap! Miles leaned his head back. A close one.

"No more thinking you're human."

Miles struggled, did his best to try to defend himself, but the snapping claws kept coming, so he had no choice but to pull his punches.

"I mean, come on, Miles." *Snap!* "You know the school mantra: *vision is at the center of all we do.* So how come you can't see that you don't belong here? That your place is in a dark corner with the flies, spider-boy. You're a nuisance, and you were born to be stepped on."

Tobin kept yanking Miles, yanking and yanking, hard enough for the sockets of Miles's legs to feel like they could catch fire any moment. On top of all this, the other termites were crawling up the walls. *All* the walls.

So, in an effort to save himself, Miles cut the web.

TO FALL

No one ever gets used
to falling. The feeling
of air leaving the
body too fast and air
entering the body
too fast at the same
time cancel each
other, out of breath.

While plummeting what had to be about thiry or forty feet, Tobin
lost his clinch on Miles's foot and landed on the ground. Falling,
Miles, twisting in the air, was able to come down on Tobin's back.

"Now it's my turn," Miles said, pounding his fists into Tobin's
abdomen. But it didn't seem to be doing much damage. Tobin didn't
seem fazed at all. So Miles reached up and grabbed Tobin's antennae.
Ripped them from his head, like he'd seen Ms. Shine pull roots from
her flower beds. Tobin screeched and whipped his massive head,
frantically knocking against the wood remnants that surrounded
them. While Tobin was thrashing, Miles slipped one of the antennae
around the giant termite's neck and pulled back, as if snatching the
reins of a horse. Tobin shuffled on his arms and legs, scattering with
Miles still on his back, holding on tight.

VIOLENCE

I didn't know termites
moved like bulls, banging,
in fury, their heads against
this world they've eaten
themselves into, this mess
of dust and splinter.

I didn't know they could
be so violent. But anything
that will destroy the pages of
a book will certainly have
no problem turning
a building into eggshell.

Miles was being tossed about and was running out of steam. He had no choice but to use his Venom Blast, which is when he draws all the electricity in his body and concentrates it into a single surge to shock and stun whomever he transfers it to. It's like harnessing lightning. Controlling its power and pattern. He doesn't use it often because it takes so much out of him, but sometimes it's necessary. And this was one of those times, especially since he was short a web-shooter. Other giant termites, not the size of Tobin—he was *giant* giant—but nasty critters the size of Miles's feet, were climbing up Miles's arms and legs, some even leaping onto *his* back, perhaps searching for *his* antennae.

"Ah!" he grunted as the termites pinched him. He was trying to shake them off while holding on to Tobin's neck as tight as he could, the termites making up Tobin's face crawling all over each other in a fit.

"Might as well give it up, Miles," Tobin scoffed. "There's no killing us. We're in the dust of this place. We *are* the dust of this place."

VENOM BLAST

It feels like
everything about me,

my Brooklyn,
my big mouth,
the car horns,
the grind and screech
against the third rail,
the sirens and lights
in the eyes of the
people who work
and wait on wings,

are all in lightning bolts
etched in the palms
of these hands.

———————

Miles charged up, and charged up, and charged up and up and up, until . . . BLAST! The electrical current pulsed through Tobin, causing him to lurch, almost as if his insides could jump out of his exoskeleton. The blast waved out beyond Tobin and spread in pulsing rings from Miles. It catapulted Miles from the giant termite's back, landing him in a pile of rubble. Quickly, Miles went into camouflage mode and disappeared himself.

INVISIBLE

The thing about
being invisible is

you don't have to run,

but you never feel
like you shouldn't.

Because you think

they can see you, that
they know you're there.

But they don't. And do.

———————

Miles moved slowly through the rubble, trying not to crack any
wood under his feet. He saw the remnants of books that had been
destroyed, the pages eaten through.

Why these? he thought. *Why are these books the ones the termites attack?*
Some Miles had read, others he'd heard about. Even copies of some
of the books Alicia had sitting on her desk.

MADE ME THINK OF MY FATHER

I wonder if the reason my father
tried so hard to keep me
from Uncle Aaron is because
my uncle, though a smudged man,
was my father's cleanest mirror
and could show me who my father
was, who he is, the him he wrestles
down every morning to be Dad.

AND MY MOTHER

Whenever we have steak,
she tells me that when the cooking
is over, it's best to ignore what we
have made for a while. *It's best
to let it rest* is the way she puts it,
because it's rare, so if you don't,
it'll bleed all over everything,
and no one wants to be reminded,
at least not like that, that they're
eating a thing that was once alive.

"Where are you, Miles?" Tobin growled, shaking off the stun. He banged his head against the wall. Snapped his mandible. The birth-mark of termite still moving around his face, feeding feeding feed-ing on him. "I know you're here."

Miles froze, held his breath, staring down at the scraps of a book. Its cover not completely tattered: *The Fire Next Time.*

Tobin crawled around, swinging from left to right. "You know, Miles, not every book is meant to exist. Just because a person has a story doesn't mean it needs to live in the world. There are right stories and there are wrong ones, and we're just making sure there's space for the right ones. You can understand that, can't you?"

HMM

I wonder if
my mother's story matters.
Mi abuela in Loíza.
My father's story.
My uncle's story.
My cousin's story.

I wonder if
Alicia's story matters.
Or Ganke's story.
His Korean American parents'.
Or Neek's story of war.
Or Martell's of sport.

I wonder if
the stories of the barbershop matter.
Or the ones that spill out.
The bodega tales
and the ones caught
between the lips of bench-kissers.

I wonder if
my story matters.
Or is it meant to be
pulled from the shelf,
pages ripped from the spine,
gnawed and nah'd?

———————

"Which ones are the *right* ones?" Miles asked, already on his toes.

Tobin didn't bother responding, just pounced toward the sound of Miles's voice. Miles leapt right over him, and Tobin belly flopped into the wreckage, thick dust kicking up around them.

Miles tried to fan it away but couldn't.   His nose started to itch.

Oh no.

ACHOO!

_____

And just like that, Miles reappeared, the camouflage interrupted by . . . a sneeze.

"Ah! There you are!" Tobin growled.

Then he shot off after Miles, who tried leaping toward one of the walls but was swatted down. As soon as Miles got to his feet, Tobin swiped at him, his thorny hands slicing Miles's face. Blood.

On his back, backing up, Miles was in trouble.

Tobin's pincers were coming in. Closer. Closer. They'd pierced through pages of a book, someone's story kabobbed on the ends of the nippers.

"There will always be Wardens. And Chamberlains. Even when you think they're gone. You can't kill us all!" Tobin thrusted toward Miles, but instead of Tobin snapping his face, Miles blocked it with his wrist, his fist now in Tobin's mouth, the mandible locked around his flesh, but not the metal of Miles's web-shooter.

"Maybe you're right," Miles said, shaking his head. "But at least there will be one less."

-..-. . -. ... --- .-. ... .--. / .. ... / - ....
. / -.-. ....-.. -.. / --- ..-. / ..-. . .- .-. /
.- -. -.. / - .... . / ..-. .- - .... . .-. / --- ..-.
/ .. --. -. --- .-. .- -. -.-. . / -.-. . -. ... ---
.-. ... .--. / .. ... / - .... . / -.-. ....-..
-.. / --- ..-. / ..-. . .- .-. / .- -. -.. / - .... .
/ ..-. .- - .... . .-. / --- ..-. / .. --. -. --- .-.
.- -. -.-. . / -.-. . -. ... --- .-. ... .--. /
.. ... / - .... . / -.-. ....-.. -.. / --- ..-. / ..-.
. .- .-. / .- -. -.. / - .... . / ..-. .- - .... . .-.
/ --- ..-. / .. --. -. --- .-. .- -. -.-. . / -.-. .
-. ... --- .-. ... .--. / .. ... / - .... . / -.-.
....-.. -.. / --- ..-. / ..-. . .- .-. / .- -. -..
/ - .... . / ..-. .- - .... . .-. / --- ..-. / .. --.
-. --- .-. .- -. -.-. . / -..-. . -. ... --- .-. ... .
.. .--. / .. ... / - .... . / -.-. ....-.. -.. / ---
..-. / ..-. . .- .-. / .- -. -.. / - .... . / ..-. .- -
.... . .-. / --- ..-. / .. --. -. --- .-. .- -. -.-. . .

Miles emptied the cartridge. Pumped web onto Tobin's face, focusing primarily on the moving birthmark: the tiny termites nibbling on Tobin. Feeding on him. Covering the majority of his face like a mask. He layered the web, thicker and thicker, almost turning it into a paste. And when the shooter sputtered to its end, Miles gripped the web, and yanked the termites from Tobin's skin.

Without the termites there, Tobin's face and body—at least this version of him—became . . . wood. Eaten through. Hollowed out. And Tobin—at least this version of him—fell to the ground just like the tree Miles had avoided outside the library earlier in the day. And broke into pieces.

CLANG CLANG, KNOCK KNOCK!

BELL!

END OF DAY

SPIDER FACT

There is a special
species of spider,

ammoxenus,
that's fascinating because

they're the only animal
predator on the planet

with a diet consisting
of a single species.

On the menu: termites.
Just termites.

———————

And as the termites around Miles escaped back into the dark hiding places, there were limbs left over. Jagged driftwood. Miles picked one up, a log like an arm, and knew—this wasn't Tobin. And was relieved.

OVER

I hobble back through
the gutted corridor
behind the wall,

over the hurdles
and hindrances,
before returning

to the hole in the stall.
Rip the web from the door,
open it to find

no one.
Brewton had left.
His boots had not.

As the hall flooded with students murmuring jokes about *the monsters behind the wall,* Miles limped back toward Room 501, his cuffs unbuttoned, his shirt untucked. On the way there, just up the hall, he spotted Tobin. He looked bad, and was being held up by Mr. Chamberlain.

MR. CHAMBERLAIN WITH TOBIN E. ROGERS: A DESCRIPTION

Imagine a ball player,
one who's good with trick moves,
spinning a basketball on their finger
like a world, slapping it so it might spin
faster and faster, taunting the onlookers
about how it couldn't be lost, it couldn't
slip from fingertip to floor, and even if
it did, the ball would bounce right back
into the trickster's grasp.

Now imagine that ball is a boy.
Now imagine that boy is a bomb.

———————

Though kids are everywhere in the hallway, Miles was able to spot Reggie. Reggie was still putting posters up. About a protest. About books that need to be available in the library.

"You know what happened to him?" Miles asked Reggie as Mr. Chamberlain and Tobin doddered toward them. Tobin held his glasses in his hand, and when he caught eyes with Miles, he nodded, slightly. Then Tobin slapped something off his arm. Something that Miles didn't have to see to know what it was.

"He's sick."

"What you mean, he's sick?"

Reggie never turned away from the task. "All I know is, right when the bell rang, he came busting out the door, puking everywhere. It was gross."

"But he's okay, right?"

Reggie looked at Miles, then looked down the hall at Tobin and Mr. Chamberlain, then back at Miles. "Looks like it." Reggie shrugged. "My guess is something he ate didn't agree with his system. Just couldn't make it to the bathroom in time. It was a mess," they said, moving on, disappearing into the crowd.

Miles thought of his mother and what she'd always tell him: *A mess ain't nothing but a message.* And Miles hoped the message was that it was over. That whatever had gotten into Tobin was now out of him. But he wasn't sure that could be the case with Mr. Chamberlain serving as his support. A support that moved more like a pickpocket than a pillar.

"Where you taking him?" Miles now asked Mr. Chamberlain as they passed.

"To see the nurse, and to call his parents." Mr. Chamberlain paused, lunged toward Miles, just above his head, and snatched one of Reggie's posters down. He grimaced as if he'd puke next. "Where else would I be taking him, *Mr. Morales?*"

HISTORY CLASS
MR. MORALES i.e., A BIGMOUTH, A TROUBLE, A LIE, AN UNGRATEFUL MESS, A SNOWFLAKE, A BRAT

You ever had
a teacher

who gave teaching,
a bad name

by calling students
bad names?

(Yeah. Me too.)

———————

The janitor had already put the puke powder down outside Room 501 by the time Miles made it back. So, thankfully, he wasn't greeted by what looked like a splatter of thick ink with chunks of paper peppered in. Instead, Miles was greeted by RESPONSIBILITY and Alicia pretending to pack her bags, dawdling.

"I was . . . Ganke was waiting for you," she stammered. "What happened to your face?! You okay?" Alicia tried to nudge his chin to get a better look, but Miles pulled away, nodded, grabbed his bag, and noticed his classwork packet had been taken from his desk.

"Coach Holt took it," Alicia said.

"Okay." Miles put his hand in his bag, slipped the web shooter from his wrist, then zipped the bag shut. He wiped his face, tried to straighten himself up.

"Ain't you glad this day is over?" Alicia said, not sure what was going on or what had happened. She slung her bag onto her shoulder. "I know I am."

"Me too," Miles said, still upset about everything that had happened, and also concerned about Tobin. Hoping whatever spell Mr. Chamberlain had put on him was broken.

"So . . . where you 'bout to go?"

"To the library," Miles said.

"Oh, perfect. I have to go there, too, to return these." She held up the books that had been sitting on her desk all day.

"How long have you had those?" Miles asked, curious about their condition.

"Oh, these are way past due. Like, so late that I'm embarrassed to tell you. Wouldn't want you to think less of me and then bail on coming uptown for pizza," Alicia said.

Miles, though on a mission and still wound up, smiled.

He'd finally found the light that lifted his chin.

WITH LIMP AND CUT

My mother
will probably

say I'm hungry.

And if she does,
she'd be right.

When Miles and Alicia made it to the library, Brad Canby was already
there talking to Mrs. Tripley.

"I'm just asking you to check. I'm not saying something's wrong with these, I'm just saying maybe you should run some tests or some-thing," he said, flipping through the pages of his history textbook.

"Don't you have basketball practice?" Mrs. Tripley replied. She was tending to the classics, dusting them off and making sure they were all in order. And they were. They were perfect. Not a scratch. Not a bend. Not a tear. *Don Quixote. The Adventures of Huckleberry Finn. Frankenstein.*

"Yeah, yeah. And I'm going as soon as you admit that maybe our textbooks need to be trashed."

"Listen, Brad, as much as I'd love to help you out, there are a few reasons I can't. The first is, textbooks have nothing to do with the library. And the second is, Tobin was, let's just say, stretching the truth."

Mrs. Tripley noticed Miles and Alicia come in. She ran her hand across *Dracula.* "Ah, two more of you. What y'all do, decide this would be your meeting place after ISS? This is your happy hour? If so, I'm happy to have you, especially after what *you* did for me earlier."

"Mrs. Tripley, something's wrong," Miles said, disregarding her gratitude simply because it made him uncomfortable.

"Something's always wrong, son. That's how we know something's always right." She was always saying stuff like this. But now wasn't the time for her hippie philosophies. "Now, before I forget, what were you asking me about starting a book drive?" She lifted the *Dracula* book up. "I want to talk to you about it."

But Miles had already walked off. Without even realizing it, he'd grabbed Alicia by the hand and was leading her down the stacks.

"What book drive, Miles?" Alicia asked. But Miles didn't answer.

"What's one of your favorite books?"

"Huh?"

"Alicia, what's one of *your* favorite books?"

PATTERNS

I'm only here
looking for the truth.

The Autobiography of Malcolm X: chewed through
The Bluest Eye: chewed through
The Color Purple: chewed through
The Hate U Give: chewed through
All Boys Aren't Blue: chewed through
Speak: chewed through
Catch-22: chewed through
Fun Home: chewed through
I Know Why the Caged Bird Sings: chewed through

And on and on.

TERMITES

When I show Mrs. Tripley
the pulverized books, the first
thing she says is that she owes Tobin
an apology.   (She doesn't.)

The second thing she says is that
we need to get out of the library
immediately and that it needs to
be fumigated.   (It does.)

The third thing she says is
that Alicia can keep the books
she checked out. That they are
better with her.   (They are.)

———————

"Everybody out!" Mrs. Tripley said. "Yes, that means you, too, Brad.
I need to get all this straightened out. We'll have to fumigate this
whole building. Shoot, we may need to fumigate the whole school!"

"1-800-ALL-GONE!" Brad shouted as he exited.

SPIDER FACT

It's said
that nobody
is ever more
than ten feet
from a spider.

They be everywhere
you and me are.

When I say this
to Alicia, I'm
hoping she
says something
like, *ten feet*
is too far.

But she doesn't.
She just listens.

Until admitting
she's scared to
death of them,
but wants to know
more about the
weird world
in one's web.

Miles and Alicia sat on the fountain, watching as the day drifted into dorm rooms and study sessions, sports practices and goof-offs. Ganke, one of the goof-offs, after realizing Miles and Alicia were together talking, decided to give them some privacy. But not before walking around the fountain a few times to make things awkward.

"Hey, so, spiders are interesting and everything, but what's the deal with this book drive?" Alicia asked. Dean Kushner came power walking across the quad toward the library. Mrs. Tripley must've called him. He glanced at Miles and Alicia and, instead of speaking, just shook his head.

Miles cracked his knuckles, rolled his neck. His body slowly stiffening due to the fight with Tobin. He knew he'd really feel it in the morning. "It's for the youth prison."

"Like, you really gon' try to do it?" Alicia asked.

"My cousin's locked up," Miles said plainly. His phone buzzing in his pocket. A text message from his mother.

"Damn. I been there with some of my folks. It's rough. What's his name?"

Another text message, this one from his father. He didn't bother opening the messages, knew they were both just checking to make sure he'd made it through the day. And to tell him they loved him.

"Austin. Been in for a while, and I think he's got a while to go. So I want to make sure he and everybody in there got books, y'know? Try to read and write themselves free."

Alicia nodded. Reached into her bag and pulled out those same library books. The ones she'd had in class. The ones Mrs. Tripley let her keep.

Baldwin. Bambara. Baraka.

"You wanna start with these?" she said, scooting just a bit closer.

A KISS

ahem

On the cheek. Sandalwood.

Made him feel like all the air in his body had joined the wind. Made him feel like all the teeth in his mouth had gone gummy. Just like in his dream.

His mother always said when you dream of your teeth falling out, it's a sign of a relationship ending. Of you losing someone. But maybe when they don't fall out, when they just become soft, that's the sign of something else. Something new. Something changing. Maybe. Either way:

Miles Morales has had
        quite a day.

ACKNOWLEDGMENTS

Writing this was fun. But also really difficult. So it's definitely necessary to dole out a few *thank-yous* to the folks who helped this strange idea come to life. First and foremost, my mother and father. I almost never thank them in the acknowledgment sections of my books, but now that my father has died, I realize just how much of my imagination and courage and foolishness come from being Isabell and Allen Reynolds's child. They raised me to be wild. To be free. Most importantly, to be me.

I also have to thank Elena Giovinazzo for always going to bat for me (keep swingin'!), and Caitlyn Dlouhy for never wavering despite how far-fetched my ideas might be. We have a true partnership. And I'm always grateful to work with you to bring these stories to the world.

But this particular book is a bit different because it's, obviously, Miles Morales, who, obviously, is Spider-Man. Therefore, I would be remiss if I didn't thank all the good folks at Marvel, especially Lauren, Caitlin, Dan, and Sven, who got behind this and gave me the freedom to make what I wanted to make. Thank you for trusting me. It's been an honor to be part of this legacy in such a unique way. I'm sure to most, this will be the coolest thing I ever make.

And lastly, to all my friends who write fantasy and science-fiction, my comrades with the most expansive imaginations on Earth, who can write worlds into existence in a way I could never. You all sparked this. No, it's not the same. I know that. And yes, I'm talking about you, Dhonielle, and Zoraida, and all the rest of y'all I argue with all the time. I don't know if I got it right. But I'm inspired, and I hope after reading this, you are too.